EVIL GROWS

Evil Grows

& Other Thrilling Tales

Loren D. Estleman

Introduction copyright © 1993/2012 by Loren D. Estleman
"Evil Grows" copyright © 2001 by Mysterious Press. First appeared in *Flesh & Blood* edited by Max Allan Collins & Jeff Gelb.
"Flash" copyright © 2001 New Millennium Press. First appeared in *Murder on the Ropes*.
"How's My Driving?" copyright © 2008 Dell Magazines, a Division of Crosstown Publications. First appeared in *Alfred Hitchcock's Mystery Magazine*, January/February 2008.
"The Pioneer Strain" copyright © 1977 by Davis Publications, Inc.. First appeared in *Alfred Hitchcock's Mystery Magazine*.
"The Used" copyright © 1982 by Davis Publications, Inc.. First appeared in *Alfred Hitchcock's Mystery Magazine*.
"The Tree on Execution Hill" copyright © 1977 by Davis Publications, Inc.. First appeared in *Alfred Hitchcock's Mystery Magazine*.
"Lock, Stock, and Casket" copyright © 1982 by Loren D. Estleman. First appeared in *Pulpsmith*.
"Bad Blood" copyright © 1986 by Davis Publications, Inc.. First appeared in *Alfred Hitchcock's Mystery Magazine*.
"State of Grace" copyright © 1988 by Loren D. Estleman. First appeared in *An Eye For Justice*.
"Diminished Capacity" copyright © 1982 by Davis Publications, Inc.. First appeared in *Alfred Hitchcock's Mystery Magazine*.
"Cabana" copyright © 1990 by Loren D. Estleman. First appeared in *The Armchair Detective*.

ISBN: 979-8-3372-0145-0

This edition published in 2025 by Open Road Integrated Media, Inc.
180 Maiden Lane
New York, NY 10038
www.openroadmedia.com

CONTENTS

INTRODUCTION

William Faulkner, perhaps the least-read and most-often cited of literary pundits, said that he turned to writing novels because he found writing short stories too hard.

Although it's difficult to imagine that writing *anything* would be harder than reading Faulkner, there is truth in the statement. At its best, the short story is an exquisite miniature in which the presence of a flaw advertises itself instantly, a fact that has frightened many an established novelist away from the short form. The work is intense, the monetary reward small, and given the ephemeral nature of the periodical numbers in which the stories appear, they will likely go to their recycling-bin graves without a single review to mark their passing.

Why, then, does the writer bother? For the same reason he writes at all, for if wealth and acclaim were his chief aspirations he'd do better to sell drugs and take guitar lessons: he does it because he wants to know if he can. The best artists, from Poe and Tolstoy to Hemingway and Cheever, did their finest and most personally satisfying work under 10,000 words, and confessed that they wrote books only for leverage with which to twist their publishers' arms until they agreed to publish collections. Indeed, the beginning of the deterioration in the work of all the above-mentioned writers began when they turned their backs on the short form.

Many readers profess a dislike for short stories. Invariably they prefer fat bestsellers by former Hollywood writers to *The Great Gatsby* and windy TV miniseries sprawled over several nights to the taut thirty-minute dramas of the 1950s. Having denied themselves cholesterol at mealtimes, they demand it in their reading, not realizing that they are clogging their cortexes with the same lethal substance. (This may explain the wide acceptance of bad punctuation and spelling errors in professional printed signs such as EMPLOYEE'S ONLY and BY ORDER OF THE FIRE MARSHALL.) Their conversation is as flatulent as their taste in literature and one would do as well to discuss Congress with a cow.

The short story has been on the endangered list since Poe invented it. Yet it has managed to survive several Great Depressions, the paper shortages of a hundred wars, the decline of the great fiction magazines, and countless censorship successes from Joe McCarthy to the Ladies' Tuesday Afternoon Society for the Preservation of Decency and the Presbyterian Church, while other forms, including poetry and the novella, have gone beyond this pale. Obviously it serves some fundamental need, if indeed need has anything to do with art, whose chief attribute seems to be that it is the first thing we can do without when money is scarce.

I make no pretense that the stories that follow, dependent as they are upon the chaos that gnaws constantly at the edge of order, compare favorably with the work of the great names conjured by this introduction. Unedited from their original appearances in print, they represent my development over the past fifteen years in a straighter line than my book-length work could provide; and I hope they bear witness to the fact that I feel a certain sense of accomplishment when I finish writing a good short story that I've never gotten from any of my novels.

—Loren D. Estleman

EVIL GROWS

No, I'm not prejudiced. Well, not any more than the majority of the population. I'm an organic creature, subject to conditioning and environment, and as such I'm entitled to my own personal set of preconceptions. No, I'm not disappointed; relieved is the word. If you'd shown up with cauliflower ears or swastikas tattooed on your biceps, the interview would have been over right then. So let's sit down and jabber. What do you drink? Excuse me? Jack and Coke? Don't get defensive, you're young, you'll grow out of it. You grew out of your formula. Miss, my friend will have a Jack and Coke, and you can pour me another Chivas over rocks and don't let it sit too long on the bar this time. Scotch-flavored Kool-Aid is not my drink.

What's that? No, I'm not afraid she'll spit in my glass. She's got miles on her, no wedding ring, she needs this job. People will put up with what they have to, up to a point. Which is the point where my job begins. Or began. See, I'm not sure I'm still employed. It isn't like I go to the office every day and can see if my name's still on the door. I'm talking too much; that's my third Scotch the barmaid's spitting in. You don't mind that I'm a motor mouth? I forgot; you're one of the new breed. You want to know why. I'm down with that. Thank you, miss. Just keep the tab going.

Let's see. You ever watch the news, read a paper? Don't bother, the question's out of date. You can't avoid the news. The wise man on the mountain in Tibet picks up Dan Rather in his fillings. But that's network; it's the local reports I'm talking about, the police beat. I know what you're thinking. Crime's the last thing I should be interested in when I get home. Truth is, I can't relate to wars in Eastern Europe, not since I got too old for the draft, but give me a carjacking two streets over from where I live and you can't pry me away from the screen. Past forty you get selective about what you take in. I'm not just talking about your stomach.

Anyway, have you ever noticed, once or twice a month there's a story about some schnook getting busted trying to hire a hit man? Some woman meets a guy in a bar and offers him like a thousand bucks to knock off her husband or boyfriend or her husband's girlfriend or the mother of the girl who's beating out her daughter for captain of the cheerleading squad? Okay, it's not always a woman, but let's face it, they're still the designated child-bearers, it's unnatural for them to take a life. So they engage a surrogate. The reason they get caught is the surrogate turns out to be an undercover cop. I mean, it happens so often you wonder if there aren't more cops out there posing as hit men than there are hit men. Which may be true, I don't know. Assassins don't answer the census.

That's how it seems, and the department's just as happy to let people think that. Actually there's very little happenstance involved. The woman's so pissed she tells her plans to everyone she knows and a few she doesn't, gets a couple of margaritas in her and tells the bartender. Working up her courage, see, or maybe just talking about it makes her feel better, as if she went ahead and did it. So in a week or so twenty people are in on the secret. Odds are pretty good one of them's a cop. I don't know a bookie who'd bet against at least one of them telling a cop. So the next Saturday night she's sitting in a booth getting blasted and a character in a Harley jacket with Pennzoil in his hair slides in, buys her a zombie and a beer for himself, and says I understand you're looking for someone to take care of a little problem. Hey, nothing's subtle in a bar. People want their mechanics to be German and their decorators gay, and when they decide to have someone iced they aren't going to hire someone who looks like Hugh Grant.

You'll be happy to hear, if you're concerned about where civilization is headed, that many of these women, once they realize what's going on, are horrified. Or better yet, they laugh in the guy's face. These are the ones that are just acting out. The only blood they intend to draw will be in a courtroom, if it ever gets that far; a lot of couples who considered murder go on to celebrate their golden anniversaries. A good cop, or I should say a good person who is a cop, will draw away when he realizes it's a dry hole. It's entrapment if he pushes it, and anyway what's the point of removing someone from society who was never a threat to begin with? It just takes time away from investigations that might do some good. Plus he knows the next woman whose table he invites himself to will probably take him up on it.

Hell yes, he's wearing a wire, and I'm here to tell you Sir Laurence Olivier's got nothing on an undercover stiff who manages to appear natural knowing he can't squirm around or even lift his glass at the wrong time because the rustle of his clothing might drown out the one response he needs to make his case. I was kidding about the Harley jacket; leather creaks like a bitch, on tape it sounds like a stand of giant sequoias making love, and you don't want to hear about corduroy or too much starch in a cotton shirt. Even when you wear what's right and take care, you need to find a way to ask the same question two or three times and get the same answer, just for insurance. Try and pull that off without tipping your mitt. I mean, everyone's seen NYPD Blue. So you begin to see, as often as these arrests make the news, the opportunity comes up oftener yet You can blame Hollywood if you like, or maybe violent video games. I'm old enough to remember when it was comic books. My old man had a minister when he was ten who preached that Satan spoke through Gangbusters on the radio. My opinion? We've been fucking killers since the grave.

Lest you think I draw my munificent paycheck hanging around gin mills hitting on Lizzie Borden, I should tell you life undercover most of the time is about as exciting as watching your car rust. When the lieutenant told me to meet this Rockover woman I'd been six weeks raking leaves in the front yard of a druglord in Roseville, posing as a gardener. I never saw the man; he's in his bedroom the whole time, flushing out his kidneys and playing euchre. He's got maybe a year to live, so assuming I do gather enough for an indictment, he'll be in hell trumping Tupac's hand by the time they seat the jury. I don't complain when I'm pulled off. Friend, I'd work Stationary Traffic if it meant getting out of those goddamn overalls.

The briefing's a no-brainer. This Nola Rockover has had it with her boss. He's a lawyer and a sexual harasser besides, it's a wonder the Democrats haven't tapped him for the nomination. It's her word against his, and he's a partner in the firm, so you know who's going to come out on the short end if she reports him. Her career's involved. Admit it; you'd take a crack at him yourself. That's how you know it's worth investigating. The odd thing, one of the odd things about getting a conviction is the motive has to make sense. Some part of you has to agree with the defendant in order to hang him. It's a funny system.

Getting ready for a sting you've got to fight being your own worst enemy. You can't ham it up. I've seen cops punk their hair and pierce their noses—Christ, their tongues and belly buttons too—and get themselves tossed by a nervous bouncer before they even make contact, which is okay because nine times out of ten the suspect will take one look at them and run for the exit. I know what I said about bars and subtlety, but they're no place for a cartoon either. So what I do is I leave my hair shaggy from the gardening job, pile on a little too much mousse, go without shaving one day, put on clean chinos and combat boots and a Dead T-shirt—a little humor there, it puts people at ease and mostly for my own benefit I clip a teeny gold ring onto my left earlobe. You have to look close to see it doesn't go all the way through, I've spent every day since the academy trying to keep holes out of me and I'm not about to give up for one case. Now I look like an almost-over-the-hill Deadhead who likes to hip it up on weekends, a turtleneck and sport coat on Casual Friday is as daring is he gets during the week. Point is not so much to look like a hit man as in not look like someone who isn't. Approachability's important.

The tech guy shaves a little path from my belt to my solar plexus, tapes the mike and wire flat, the transmitter to my hack just above the butt-crack. The T's loose and made of soft cotton washed plenty of times. Only competition I have to worry about is the bar noise. Fortunately, the Rockover woman's Saturday night hangout is a family-type place, you know, where a kid can drink a Coke and munch chips from a little bag while his parents visit with friends over highballs. Loud drunks are rare, there's a Julie but no band. The finger's a co-worker in the legal firm. I meet him at the bar, he points her out, I thank him and tell him to blow. First I have to reassure him I'm not going to throw her on the floor and kneel on her back and cuff her like on Cops;

he's more worried she'll get herself in too deep than about what she might do to the boss. I go along with this bullshit and he leaves. Chances are he's got his eye on her job, but he hasn't got the spine not to feel guilty about it.

The place is crowded and getting noisy, the customers are starting to unwind. I order a Scotch and soda, heavy on the fizz, wait for a stool, and watch her for a while in the mirror. She's sitting facing another woman near the shuffleboard table, smoking a cigarette as long as a Bic pen and nursing a clear drink in a tall glass, vodka and tonic probably. I'm hoping I'll catch her alone sometime during the evening, maybe when the friend goes to the can, which means I don't count on getting any evidence on tape until I convince her to ditch the friend.

So I wait and watch, which in this case is not unpleasant. Nola Rockover's a fox. Not, I hasten to add, one of those assembly-line beauties on the order of Heather Locklear or some other blond flavor of the month, but the dark, smoldering kind you hardly ever see except in black-and-white movies and old TV shows. She's a brunette, slender—not thin, I've had it with these anorexic bonepiles that make you want to abduct them and tie them down and force-feed them mashed potatoes until they at least cast a decent shadow—I'm talking lithe and sinuous, like a dancer, with big dark eyes and prominent cheekbones. You're too young to remember Mary Tyler Moore on The Dick Van Dyke Show. I know you've seen her on Nick at Nite, but your generation's got some fixation on color, so I'm betting you're thinking about that thing she did in the seventies. You had to have seen her in capri pants and a pullover to understand what I'm getting at. If you were a man or a boy, you fell in lust with that innocent female panther, and she was all yours. I mean, you knew she was beautiful, but you thought you were the only one in the world who knew it. Well, that was Nola Rockover.

She was sitting there in this dark sleeveless top and some kind of skirt, no cleavage or jewelry except for a thin gold necklace that called your attention to the long smooth line of throat, and she had a way of holding her chin high, almost aloof but not quite, more like she hadn't forgotten what her mother had told her about the importance of good posture. She's not talking, except maybe to respond to something the other woman is saying, encourage her to go on, except I'm thinking she's not really that interested, just being polite. In any case it's her friend who's flapping her chin and waving her hands around like she's swatting hornets. Probably describing her love life.

Yes, miss, another Chivas, and how's yours? Sure? Now you're making me look like a lush.

Nola's friend? Okay, so I'm a chauvinist pig. Maybe she's talking about the Red Wings. She's got on this ugly business suit with a floppy bow tie, like she hasn't been to see a movie since *Working Girl*, jogs, drinks bottled water by the gallon and two percent milk, got enough calcium in her you could snap her like a stick. Takes the *Cosmo* quiz on the G spot. One of those goddamn silly women you see walking in sheer hose and scruffy tennis shoes, poster child for penis envy. I'm giving you a better picture of her than Nola, and I never saw her again or learned her name. I'm thinking Nola tolerates her company to avoid drinking alone in public. Maybe she already suspects she's said too much in that condition. You can see I'm kindly disposed to her before I even make contact. There's no rule saying you can't like 'em and cuff 'em. I get Christmas cards, sincere ones from killers and pushers I sent to Jackson. Meanwhile I don't know a lawyer I'd go out for lunch with, and we're supposed to be on the same side.

I watch twenty minutes, my drink's all melted ice, and I'm starting to think this other woman's got a bladder the size of

Toledo when she gets up and goes to wee-wee. I give it a minute so as not to look like a shark swimming in, then I wander on over. Nola's getting out another cigarette and I'm wishing, not for the first time, I didn't give up the weed, or I could offer to light her up from the Zippo I no longer carried. Sure, it's corny, but it works. That's how some things stay around long enough to get corny. So I do the next best thing and say, "I hear the surgeon general frowns on those."

She looks up slowly like she knows I've been standing there the whole time, and you'll like what she says. "I don't follow generals' orders any more. I got my discharge." And she smiles, this cool impersonal number that in a book would be a page of dialogue about what a load of crap the mating ritual is, and why can't we be more like cats and get right down to the scratching and yowling. Either that or she's saying go fuck yourself. I'm not sure because I'm too busy noticing what nice teeth she has—not perfect, one incisor's slightly crooked, but she keeps them white, which is not easy when you smoke, and it's good to know there's someone with the self-confidence to refuse to send some ortho-dontist's kid to Harvard just to look like a model in a tooth-paste ad. Her eyes don't smile, though. Even if I didn't know her recent history I'd guess this was someone for whom life had not come with greased wheels.

I'm scraping my skull for what to say next when she throws me a life preserver. "You like the Dead?"

Copy that. Not, "You're a Deadhead?" Which is a term they know in Bowling Green by now, it's hip no more, but most people are afraid not to use it for fear of appearing unhip. The way she doesn't say it, though, tells me she's so hip she doesn't even bother to think about it. I admit that's a lot to get out of four words, but that was Nola, a living tip-of-the-iceberg. Thanks, honey; I like my Scotch good and orange.

I lost the thread. Oh, right, the Dead. I take a chance. Remember everything hangs on how I broach the subject, and the conventional wisdom is never, ever jump the gun. If opening it up standing in front of her table with her friend about to come back any second is not jumping it, I don't know what is. I say: "I like the dead."

That was it. Lowercase, no cap. Which you may argue makes no difference when you're talking, but if you do, good day to you, because you're not the person for what I have in mind. No comment? There's hope for you. Then you'll appreciate her reaction. Her face went blank. No expression, it might have been enameled metal with the eyes painted on. She'd heard that lowercase d, knew what it meant, and quick as a switch she shut down the system. She wasn't giving me anything. Wherever this went, it was up to me to take it there.

"I know about your problem," I said. "I can help."

She didn't say, "What problem?" That would have disappointed me. Her eyes flick past my shoulder, and I know without looking her friend's coming. "Have you a card?"

This time I smile. "You mean like 'Have gun, will travel'?" She doesn't smile back. "I'm known here. I'll be at the Hangar in an hour." And then she turns her head and I'm not there.

I confer with the boys in the van, who take off their earphones long enough to agree the Hangar is Smilin' Jack's Hangar, a roadhouse up in Oakland that's been around since before that comic strip folded, a trendy spot once that now survives as a place where the laws of marriage don't apply, which is enough to pay the bills even after it gets around that it's not Stoli in the Stoli bottles but cheap Smirnoff's and that a ten-dollar bill traded for a three-fifty drink will come back as a five-spot more often than not. Every community needs a place to mess around.

So forty minutes later, wearing fresh batteries, I'm groping through the whiskey-sodden dark of a building that was once an actual hangar for a rich flying enthusiast under the New Deal, my feet not touching the floor because the bass is so deep from the juke, looking for a booth that is not currently being used for foreplay. When I find one and order my watered-down Scotch, I'm hoping Nola's part bat, because the teeny electric lamp on the table is no beacon.

No need to worry. At the end of ten minutes, right on time, I hear heels clicking and then she rustles into the facing seat. She's freshened her makeup, and with that long dark hair in an underflip and the light coming up from below leaving all the shadows where they belong, she looks like someone I wish I had a wife to cheat on with. I notice her scent: Some kind of moon-flowering blossom, dusky. Don't look for it; it wouldn't smell the same on anyone else.

"Who are you?" She doesn't even wait for drinks.

"Call me Ted."

"No good. You know both my names, and if we do this thing you'll know where I work. That's too much on your side."

I grin. "Ted Hazlett." Which is a name I use sometimes. It's close to "hazard," but not so close they won't buy it.

"And what do you do, Ted Hazlett?"

"This and that."

"Where do you live?"

"Here and there. We can do this all night if you like."

My Scotch comes. She asks for vodka tonic—I'm right about that—and when the waiter's gone she settles back and lights up one of those long cigarettes. Determining to enjoy herself.

"We're just two people talking," she says. "No law against that."

"Not according to the ACLU."

"'This and that.' Which one is you kill people?"

I think this over very carefully. "'That.'"

She nods, like it's the right answer. She tells her story then, and there's nothing incriminating in the way she tells it, at least not against her. She's a paralegal with a downtown firm whose name I knows having been cross-examined by some of its personnel in the past. Attends law school nights, plans someday to practice family law, except this walking set of genitalia she's assigned to, partner in the firm, is planning even harder to get into her pants. You know the drill: whispered obscenities in her ear when they're alone in an office, anonymous gifts of crotchless panties and front-loading bras sent to her apartment in the mail, midnight phone calls when she's too groggy to think about hitting the Record button on the machine. At first she's too scared to file a complaint, knowing there's no evidence that can be traced to him. Then comes the day he tells her she'd better go down on him if she wants a job evaluation that won't get her fired. These evaluations are strictly subjective, there's nobody in the firm you can appeal to, the decks are stacked in management's favor. The firm's as old as habeas; no rec means no legal employment elsewhere. To top it off, this scrotum, this partner, sits on the board of the school she attends and is in a position to expel her and wipe out three years of credits. Any way you look at it he's got her by the smalls.

What's a girl to do? She's no Shirley Temple, lived with a guy for two years, object matrimony, until she caught him in the shower with a neighbor and threw his clothes out a window—I mean every stitch, he had to go out in a towel to fetch them. So she does the deed on the partner, thinking to hand in her two weeks' notice the next day and take her good references to a firm where oral examinations are not required.

Except she's so good at it the slob threatens to withhold references if she refuses to assign herself to him permanently, so to speak. Sure, I could have told her too, but it's a lot easier from the sidelines. She knew the odds, but she rolled the dice anyway and came up craps.

After stewing over it all weekend, she decides to take it up with the head of the firm, file a complaint. But the senior partner won't sully himself and fobs her off on an assistant, who by the time she finishes her story has pegged her as an immoral bitch who's gone to blackmail when she found out she couldn't advance herself on her knees, if you get what I'm saying; she can see it in his face when he tells her the incident will be investigated. Next day she's assigned to computer filing. It's obvious the investigation stopped with the partner, who is now out to hound her out of the firm, filing being a notorious dead end whether it involves a modem or a bunch of metal cabinets.

But he doesn't stop there. She tries to finance a new car but gets denied for bad credit. Pulls out her card to buy a blouse at Hudson's, the clerk makes a call, then cuts up the card in front of her. Some more stuff like that happens, then late one night she gets another phone call. It's the walking genitalia, telling her he's got friends all over and if she isn't nice to him he'll phony up her employment record, get her fired, evict her, frame her for soliciting, whatever; it's him or a cell at County, followed by a refrigerator carton on Woodward Avenue, choice is hers. He's psycho, no question, but he's a psycho with connections. The refrigerator carton seals the deal. She's his now, and the law is no longer her parachute. What the partner hasn't figured on is that by blocking all the legal exits, he's left her with only one way out.

There's no way I can tell you all this the way Nola told it. She lays it out flat, just the facts, without a choke or a sob. I'm ready for the waterworks; I've seen some doozies, Oscar-quality stuff, they don't call undercover Umbrella Duty for nothing. The only hint Nola's stinging at all is when she breaks a sentence in half to sip her drink, like a runner taking a hit of oxygen before he can go on. Maybe she's just thirsty. What I'm saying is there's nothing to distract from the bare bones of her story. And I know every word's true. I can see this puffed-up fucker in his Armani, ripping up some poor schmoe in court for stepping out on his wife, then rushing back to the office for his daily quickie with the good-looking paralegal. And while I'm seeing this—I can't say even now if I knew I was doing it—I sneak a hand up under my shirt and disconnect the wire.

Nola won't talk business in a bar. She suggests we meet at her place the next night and gives me an address on East Jefferson. I stand up when she does, pay for the drinks—there's no discussion on that, it's an assumption we both make—and I go to the can, mainly to give her a chance to make some distance before I meet with the crew in the van. Only when I leave the roadhouse, I know she's somewhere out there in the dark, watching me. I walk right past the van and get into my car and pull out. I don't even give the earlobe-tug that tells them I'm being watched, because I know Nola would recognize it for what it was. And I spend an extra fifteen minutes crazying up the way home, just in case she's following me.

My telephone's ringing when I get in, and I'm not surprised it's Carpenter, from the van. What's the deal, he wants to know, something went wrong with the transmitter and you forgot we were out there freezing off our asses, you get drunk or what? I tell him I'm wiped out, sorry, I must have pulled loose a wire without knowing. Not to worry; the Nola thing didn't pan out, she was just looking for a sympathetic ear, had no intention of following up on her wish-dream of offing the partner. I didn't like the way the bartender was giving me the fish-eye, thought if I was seen climbing in and out of a van in the parking lot I might blow any chance of a future bust involving the high-stakes poker game that went on in the back room Tuesday nights. Which was the only truth I told Carpenter that night.

I don't know if he believed me about Nola, but he didn't question it Carpenter's not what you call gung ho, would just as soon duck the graveyard shift for whatever reason. It's not for fear of his disapproval I stay awake most of that night wishing I still smoked. I can still smell her cigarettes and that dusky scent on my clothes.

Most of the next day is spent filling out reports on the nonexistent Rockover Case. I log out in time to go home and freshen up and put on a sport shirt and slacks, no sense working on the image now that the hook's in. Understand, I have no intention of whacking the son of a bitch who's bringing Nola grief. In twelve years with the department I've never even fired my piece except on the range, and even if I had I'm not about to turn into Sammy the Bull for anyone. I'm sympathetic to her case, maybe I can help her figure a way out—brace the guy and apply a little strongarm if necessary, see will he pick on someone his own size and gender. Okay, and maybe wrangle myself some pussy while I'm at it. Hey, we're both single, and it's been a stretch for me, what with everyone so scared of AIDS and GHB; I'm telling you, the alphabet's played hell with the mating game. I figure I'm still leagues above the prick in the two-thousand-dollar suit.

She's on the second floor of one of those converted warehouses in what is now called Rivertown, with a view of the water through a plate-glass window the size of a garage door in her living room. Decor's sleek, all chrome and glass and black leather and a spatter of paint in a steel frame on one wall, an Impressionist piece that when you stand back turns out to be of a nude woman reclining, who looks just enough like Nola I'm afraid to ask if she posed for it. I can tell it's good, but the colors are all wrong: bilious green and violent purple and a kind of rusty brown that I can only describe as dried blood, not a natural flesh tone in the batch. It puts me in mind less of a beautiful naked woman than a jungle snake coiled around a tree limb. Just thinking about it makes my skin crawl.

It takes me a while to take all this in, because it's Nola who opens the door for me. She's wearing a dark turtleneck top with ribs over skin-tight stirrup pants with the straps under her bare feet, which are long and narrow, with high arches and clear polish on the toenails. It's as if she knows I'm a connoisseur of women's feet. With plastic surgery getting to be as common as root canals, pretty faces come four-for-a-quarter, and the effect is gone when you look down and see long bony toes with barn paint. Nola's perfect feet are just about the only skin she's showing, but I'm telling you, I'm glad I brought a bottle of wine to hold in front of myself. It's like I'm back in high school.

She takes the bottle with thanks, her eyes flicker down for a split second, and the corners of her lips turn up the barest bit, but she says nothing, standing aside to let me in and closing the door behind me, locking it with a crisp little snick. Bird Parker's playing low on a sound system I never did get to see. She has me open the wine using a wicked-looking corkscrew in the tiny kitchen, and we go to the living room and drink from stemware and munch on crackers she's set out on a tray on the glass coffee table, crumbly things that dissolve into butter on the tongue. I'm sitting on the black leather sofa, legs crossed, her beside me with hers curled under her, as supple as the snakewoman in the picture, giving off that scent. She looks even better by indirect light than she did in the Hangar. I'm thinking the Gobi at noon would be no less flattering.

We start with small talk, music and wine and the superiority of streamlined contemporary over life in a museum full of worm-eaten antiques, then she lifts her glass to her lips and asks me if I approve of the police department's retirement package.

She slides it in so smoothly I almost answer. When it hits, I get the same shuddery chill I got from the picture, only worse, like the time I had my cover blown when I'd been moled into a car theft ring downriver for a month, bunch of mean ridgerunners whose weapon of choice was a welding torch. Don't ask me why. All she's armed with is crystal.

I don't try to run a bluff, the way I did with the car thieves— successfully, I might add. Rivertown is not Downriver, and Nola Rockover is not a gang of homicidal hillbillies, although I know now they'd be a trade-up. I ask her how she doped it out.

"You forget I'm in computer filing. I ran that name you gave me through the system; you shouldn't have used one you'd used before. It came up on the transcript when you testified against one of our clients as arresting officer. Are you getting all this on tape?"

And would you believe it, there's no emotion in her tone. She might have been talking about some case at work that had nothing to do with either of us. All I see in her eyes is the reflection of the wine glass she's still holding up. I look into them and say no, I'm not wearing a wire; I was before, but I yanked it. I want to help.

"Am I supposed to believe that?"

"Lady, if it's a lie, you'd be in a holding cell right now."

Which has its effect. She drinks a little more wine, and then she leans across me to set her glass down on the table. Before I know it she's got her hands inside my sport shirt. She goes on groping long after it's obvious there's nothing under it but me. And in a little while I know there's nothing but Nola under the sweater and pants. It's like wrestling a snake, only a warm one with a quicker tongue that tastes like wine when it's in my mouth and burns like liquid fire when it's working its way down my chest, and down and down while I'm digging holes in the leather upholstery with my fingers trying to hang on.

Understand, I'm not one of these fools that regales his friends with the play-by-play. I want you to see how a fairly good cop brain melted down before Nola's heat. I was married, and I've had my hot-and-heavies, but I've never even read about some of the things we did that night. We're on the sofa, we're off the sofa, the table tips over and we're heaving away in spilled wine and bits of broken crystal; I can show you a hundred little healed-over cuts on my back even now and you'd think I got tangled in barbed wire. In a little while we're both slick with wine and sweat and various other bodily fluids, panting like a couple of wolves, and we're still going at it. I'm not sure they'd take a chance showing it on the Playboy Channel.

Miss? Oh, miss? Ice water, please. I'm burning up.

That's better. Whew. When I think about that night—hell, whenever I think about Nola—this song keeps running through my head. It isn't what Bird was playing on the record; he died years before it came out. It wasn't a hit, although it should have been, it was catchy enough. I don't even know who recorded it. "Evil Grows," I think it was called, and it was all about this poor schnook realizing his girl's evil and how every time he sees her, evil grows in him. Whoever wrote it knew what he was talking about, because by the time I crawled out of that apartment just before dawn, I'd made up my mind to kill Nola's boss for her.

His name's Ethan Hollis, and he's living beyond his means in Grosse Pointe, but if they outlaw that they'll have to throw a prison wall around the city. I don't need to park more than two minutes in front of the big Georgian he shares with his wife to know it won't happen in there, inside a spiked fence with the name of his alarm company on a sign on the front gate. Anyway, since I'm not the only one who's heard Nola's threats, we've agreed that apparent accidental death is best. I'm just taking stock. The few seconds I get to see him through binoculars, coming out on the porch to tell the gardener he isn't clipping the hedge with his little finger extended properly—I'm guessing, I can't hear him across four acres of clipped lawn—is enough to make me hate him, having worked that very job under the druglord in Roseville. He's chubbier than I had pictured, a regular teddy bear with curly dark hair on his head and a Rolex on his fat wrist, with a polo shirt, yet. He deserves to die if for no other reason than his lack of fashion sense.

I know his routine thanks to Nola, but I follow him for a week, just to look. I've taken personal time, of which I've built up about a year, undercover being twenty-four/seven. The guy logs four hours total in the office; rest of the time he's lunching with clients, golfing with the senior partner, putting on deck shoes and dorky white shorts and pushing a speedboat up and down the river, that sort of bullshit. Drowning would be nice, except I'd join him, because I can't swim and am no good with boats.

These are my days. Nights I'm with Nola, working our way through the Kama Sutra and adding footnotes of our own.

The only time I can expect Hollis to be alone without a boat involved is when he takes his Jaguar for a spin. It's his toy, he doesn't share it. Trouble is not even Nola knows when he'll get the urge. So every day when he's home I park around the corner and trot back to his north fence, watching for that green convertible. It's a blind spot to the neighbors too, and for the benefit of passersby I'm wearing a jogging suit; just another fatcat following the surgeon general's advice.

Four days in, nothing comes through that gate but Hollis's black Mercedes, either with his wife on the passenger's side or just him taking a crowded route to work or the country club.

I'm figuring I can get away with the jogging gig maybe another half a day before someone gets nervous and calls the cops, when out comes the Jag, spitting chunks of limestone off the inside curves of the driveway. I hustle back to my car. Hollis must need unwinding, because he's ten miles over the limit and almost out of sight when I turn into his street.

North is the choice today. In a little while we're up past the lake, with the subdivisions thinning out along a two-lane blacktop. It's a workday—Nola's in the office, good alibi—and for miles we're the only two cars, so I'm hanging back, but I can tell he's not paying attention to his rearview or he'd open it up and leave me in the dust. Arrogant son of a bitch thinks he's invulnerable. You see how I'm taking every opportunity to work up a good hate? I'm still not committed. I'm thinking when I get him alone I'll work him over, whisper in his ear what's in store if he doesn't lay off Nola. He's such a soft-looking slob I know he'll cave if I just knock out a tooth.

After an hour and a half we've left the blacktop and are towing twin streamers of dust down a dirt road with farms on both sides and here and there a copse of trees left for windbreaks. Now it's time to open the ball. I've got police lights installed inside the grille, and as I press down the accelerator I flip them on. Now he finds his rearview mirror, begins to slow down. But we're short of the next copse of trees, so I close in and encourage him forward, then as we enter the shade I signal him to pull over.

I've shucked the jogging suit by this time, and am wearing my old uniform. I put on my cap and get out and approach the Jag with my hand resting on the sidearm on my right hip. The window on the driver's side purrs down, he flashes his pearlies nervously. "Was I speeding, Officer?"

"Step out of the car, please."

He's got his wallet out. "I have my license and registration." I tell him again to step out of the car.

He looks surprised, but he puts the wallet away and grasps the door handle. His jaw's set I can see he thinks it's a case of mistaken identity and he may have a lucrative harassment suit if he can make himself disagreeable enough. Then his face changes again. He's looking at the uniform.

"You're pretty far out of your jurisdiction, aren't you? This area is patrolled by the county sheriff."

I repeat myself a second time, and this time I draw my sidearm.

"Fuck you, fake cop," says he, and floors it.

But it's a gravel road, and the tires spin for a second, spraying gravel, bits of which strike my legs and sting like hornets, which gives me the mad to make that lunge and grab the window post with my free hand. Just then the tread bites and the Jag spurts ahead and I know I'm going to be dragged if I don't let go or stop him.

I don't let go. I stick the barrel of my revolver through the window, cocking the hammer for the effect, and who knows but it might have worked, except my fingers slip off the window post and as I fall away from the car I strike my other wrist against the post and a round punches a hole through the windshield. Hollis screams, thinks he's hit, takes his hands off the wheel, and that's the last I see of him until after the Jag plunges into a tree by the side of the road. The bang's so loud if you even heard my revolver go off you'd forget about it because the second report is still ringing in your ears thirty seconds later, across a whole fucking field of wheat.

I get up off the ground and sprint up to the car, still holding the gun. The hood's folded like a road map, the radiator pouring steam. Hollis's forehead is leaning against the cracked steering wheel. I look up and down the road and across the field opposite the stand of trees. Not a soul in sight, if you don't count a cow looking our way. Just as I'm starting to assimilate the size of my good break, I hear moaning. Hollis is lifting his head. Lawyers are notoriously hard to kill.

His forehead's split, his face is covered with blood. It looks bad enough to finish him even if it wasn't instantaneous, but I'm no doctor. I guess you could say I panicked. I reached through the window and hit him with the butt of the revolver, how many times I don't know, six or seven or maybe as many as a dozen. The bone of his forehead started to make squishing sounds like thin ice that's cracking under your feet, squirting water up through the fissures. Only in this case it wasn't water, of course, and I know I'm going to have to burn the uniform because my gun arm is soaked to the elbow with blood and gray ooze. Finally I stop swinging the gun and feel for a pulse in his carotid. He wasn't using it any more. I holstered the revolver, took his head in both hands, and rested his squishy forehead against the steering wheel where it had struck. The windshield's still intact except for the bullet hole, so I look around and find a fallen tree limb and give it the old Kaline swing, smashing in the rest of the glass from outside. I settle the limb back into the spot where it had lain among the rotted leaves on the ground, take a last look to make sure I didn't drop anything, get into my car, and. leave, making sure first to put the jogging suit back on over my gory uniform. And only the cow is there to see me make my getaway.

For the next few days I stay clear of Nola. I don't even call, knowing she'll hear about it on the news; I can't afford anyone seeing us together. I guess I was being overcautious. Hollis's death was investigated as an accident, and at the end of a week the sheriff tells the press the driver lost control on loose gravel

I guess the cow didn't want to get involved I was feeling good about myself. I didn't see any need to wrestle with my conscience over the death of a sexual predator, and a high-price lawyer to boot. As is the way of human nature I patted my own back for a set of fortunate circumstances over which I'd had no control.

I was starting to feel God was on my side.

But Nola isn't. When I finally do visit, after the cops have paid their routine calla dn gone away satisfied her beef with her employer was unconnected with an accident upstate, she gives me hell for staying away, accuses me of cowardly leaving her to face the police alone. I settle her down finally, but I can see my explanation doesn't satisfy. As I'm taking off my coat to get comfortable she tells me she has an early morning, everyone at the firm is working harder in Hollis's absence and she needs her sleep. This is crap because Hollis was absent almost as often when he was alive, but I leave.

She doesn't answer her phone for two days after that. When I go to the apartment her bell doesn't answer and her car isn't in the port. I come back another night, same thing. I lean against the building groping in my pockets, forgetting I don't smoke anymore, then Nola's old yellow Camaro swings in off Jefferson and I step back into the shadow, because there are two people in that front seat. I watch as the lights go off and they get out.

"If you're afraid of him, why don't you call the police?" A young male voice, belonging to a slender figure in a green tank top and torn jeans.

"Because he *is* the police. Oh, Chris, I'm terrified. He won't stop hounding me this side of the grave." And saying this Nola huddles next to him and hands him her keys to open the front door, which he does one-handed, his other being curled around her waist.

They go inside, and the latch clicking behind them sounds

like the coffin lid shutting in my face. Nola's got a new shark in her school. I'm the chum she's feeding him. And I know without having to think about it that I've killed this schnook Ethan Hollis for the same reason Chris is going to kill me; I've run out of uses. So for Chris, I'm now the sexual predator.

That's why we're talking now. It's Nola or me, and I need to be somewhere else when she has her accident. I've got a feeling I'm not in the clear over Hollis. Call it cop's sense, but I've been part of the community so long I know when I've been excluded. Even Carpenter won't look me in the eye when we're talking about the flicking Pistons. I've been tagged.

Except you're not going to kill Nola, sweetie. No, not because you're a woman; you girls have moved into every other job, why not this? You're not going to do it because you're a cop.

Forget how I know. Say a shitter knows a shitter and leave it there. What? Sure, I noticed when you reached up under your blouse. I thought at the time you were adjusting your bra, but— well, that was before I said I'd decided to kill Hollis, wasn't it? I hope your crew buys it, two wires coming loose in the same cop's presence within a couple of weeks. I'll leave first so you can go out to the van and tell them the bad news. I live over on Howard. Well, you know the address. You bring the wine— no Jack and Coke—I'll cook the steaks. I think I can finish convincing you about Nola. Like killing a snake.

FLASH

Midge was glad he'd put on the electric-blue suit that day. He could use the luck.

Mr. Wassermann didn't approve of the suit. At the beginning of their professional relationship, he'd introduced Midge to his tailor, a small man in gold-rimmed glasses who looked and dressed like Mr. Wassermann, and who gently steered the big man away from the bolts of shimmering sharkskin the concern kept in stock for its gambler clients, and taught him to appreciate the subtleties of gray worsted and fawn-colored flannel. He cut Midge's jackets to allow for the underarm Glock rather than obliging him to buy them a size too large, and made his face blush when he explained the difference between "dressing left" and "dressing right."

The tailoring bills came out of Midge's salary, a fact for which he was more grateful than if the suits had been a gift. He was no one's charity case. The distinction was important, because he knew former fighters who stood in welfare lines and on street corners, holding signs saying they would work for food. Back when they were at the top of the bill, they had made the rounds of all the clubs with yards of gold chain around their necks, girls on both arms, and now here they were, saying they would clean out your gutters for a tuna sandwich, expecting pedestrians to feel guilty enough to buy them the sandwich and skip the gutters. Mr. Wassermann never gave anyone anything for nothing—it was a saying on the street, Midge had heard him confirm it in person—and the big ex-fighter was proud to be able to say in return that he never took anything from anyone for nothing.

He liked the way he looked in the suits. They complemented his height without calling attention to his bulk, did not make him look poured into his clothes the way so many of his over-developed colleagues appeared when they dressed for the street, and if it weren't for his Jagged nose and the balloons of scar tissue around his eyes, he thought he might have passed for a retired NFL running back with plenty in Wall Street. Of course, that's when he wasn't walking with Mr. Wassermann, when no one would mistake him for anything but personal security.

Today, however, without giving the thing much thought, he'd decided to wear the electric-blue double-breasted he'd worn to Mr. Wassermann's office the day they'd met. He'd had on the same shade of trunks when he KO'd Lincoln Flagg at Temple Gate Arena and again when he took the decision from Sailor Burelli at Waterworks Park. He'd liked plenty of flash in those days, in and out of the ring: gold crowns, red velvet robes with Italian silk linings, crocodile luggage, yellow convertibles. Make 'em notice you, he'd thought, and you just naturally have to do your best.

But then his run had finished. He lost two key fights, his business manager decamped to Ecuador with his portfolio, the IRS attached his beach house. The last of the convertibles went back to the finance company. In a final burst of humiliation, an Internet millionaire with dimples on his forehead bought Midge's robes at auction for his weekend guests to wear around the swimming pool When Midge had asked Mr. Wassermann for the bodyguard job, he'd been living for some time in a furnished room on Magellan Street and the electric-blue was the only suit he owned.

It had brought him luck, just as the trunks had. He'd gotten the job, and right away his fortunes turned around. Because Mr. Wassermann preferred to keep his protection close, even when it was off duty, he had moved Midge into a comfortable three-room suite in the East Wing, paid for his security training and opened an expense account for him at Rinehart's, where well-dressed salesmen advised him on which accessories to wear with his new suits and supplied him with turtle-backed hair-brushes and aftershave. On the rare occasions when his reclusive employer visited a restaurant (too many of his colleagues had been photographed in such places with their faces in their plates and bullet holes In their heads), he always asked the chef to prepare a takeout meal for Midge to eat when they returned home. These little courtesies were offered as if they were part of the terms of employment.

Because there were other bodyguards, Midge had Saturdays off, and with money in the pocket of a finely tailored suit, he rarely spent them alone. The women who were drawn to the aura of sinister power that surrounded Mr. Wassermann belonged to a class Midge could not have approached when he was a mere pug. While waiting for his employer, he would see a picture of a stunning model in *Celebrity* and remember how she looked naked in his bed at the Embassy.

There had been a long dry spell in that department after his last fight. True, his face had been stitched and swollen and hard to look at, but that wasn't an impediment after the Burelli decision, when eighteen inches of four-oh thread and a patch of gauze were the only things holding his right ear to his head; he'd made the cover of *Turnbuckle* that week and signed a contract to endorse a national brand of athlete's-foot powder. He'd considered hiring his own bodyguard to fight off the bottle-blond waitresses. But that was when he was winning. The two big losses and particularly the stench that had clung to the twelve rounds he'd dropped to Sonny Rodriguez at the Palace Garden might as well have been a well-advertised case of the clap.

The fans had catcalled and crumpled their programs and beer cups and hurled them at the contestants. The Palace management had been forced to call the police to escort them to their dressing rooms. Three weeks later, the state boxing commission had reviewed the videotape and yanked Midge's license.

The irony was, he hadn't gone Into the tank, he'd taken the money when it was offered, and since he considered himself an ethical person he'd fully intended to fake a couple of falls and force a decision against him, but he hadn't gone three rounds before he realized he was no match for the untried youngster from Nicaragua. He was out of shape and slow, and Rodriguez was graceless for all the fact that any one of his blows would have downed a young tree. Even the fellow who had approached Midge and ought to have known a fix from a legitimate loss called him afterward to tell him he was a rotten actor; he feared a congressional investigation.

Midge had considered returning the money, but that had proven to be a more complicated thing altogether than he'd suspected. He was both a fighter who had sold out and who had never thrown a fight. Just trying to think where that placed him in the scheme of things gave him a headache worse than the one he'd suffered for two weeks after he went down to Ricky Shapiro.

On this particular Saturday off, he'd broken a date with a soap opera vixen to meet a man with whom Mr. Wasserman sometimes did business. Angelo DeRiga—"Little Angie," Midge had heard him called, although he was not especially small, in fact an inch or two taller than Mr. Wassermann—dyed his hair black, even his eyebrows, and wore suits that were as well made as Midge's new ones, from material of the same good quality, but were cut too young for him. The flaring lapels and cinched waists called attention to the fact that he was nearing sixty, just as the black black hair brought out the deep lines in the artificial tan of his face. The effect was pinched and painful and increased the bodyguards appreciation for his employer's dignified herringbones and barbered white fringe.

Little Angie shook Midge's hand at the door to his the King William, complimented him upon his suit—"Flash, the genuine article," he said, and invited him to sample the gourmet spread the hotel's waiters were busy transferring from a wheeled cart to the glass-topped mahogany table in the sitting room.

Midge, who knew as well as Little Angie that the electric-blue sack was inappropriate, did not thank him, and politely refused the offer of food. He wasn't hungry, and anyway, chewing interfered with his concentration. Too many blows to the head had damaged his hearing. High- and low-pitched voices were the worst, and certain labials missed him entirely. By focusing his attention on the speaker, and with the help of some amateur lipreading, he'd managed to disguise this rather serious disability for a watchdog to have from even so observant a man as Mr. Wassermann; but then Mr. Wassermann spoke slowly, and always around the middle range. Little Angie was shrill and carried on every conversation as if it were on a fast elevator and had to finish before the car reached his floor.

When the waiters left, the two were alone with Francis, Little Angie's bodyguard. He was a former professional wrestler who shaved his head and had rehearsed his glower before a mirror until it was as nearly permanent as a tattoo. As a rule, Midge got on with other people's security, but he and Francis had disliked each other from the start. He suspected that on Francis' part this was jealousy; Mr. Wassermann's generosity to employees was well known, while Little Angie was a pinchpenny who abused his subordinates, sometimes in public. On Midge's side, he had a career prejudice against wrestlers, whom he dismissed as trained apes, and thought Francis disagreeably ugly into the bargain. When they were in the same room they spent most of the time scowling at each other. They had never exchanged so much as a word.

"I know Jake the Junkman's been white to you," Little Angie seemed to be saying. "Too good, maybe. Some types need to be put on an allowance. A lot of smart guys can't handle dough."

Midge didn't like what he'd heard. Everyone knew Mr. Wassermann had made his first fortune from scrap metal, but most respected him too much to allude to his past in this offensive way. He wondered if it was his place to report the conversation to his employer. So far he didn't know why he'd been invited here.

Little Angie reached into a pocket and took out a handful of notepaper on which Midge recognized his own scrawl. "You ain't hard to track. Everywhere you go, you leave markers: Benny Royal's floating crap game in the South Side, the roulette wheel at the Kit-Kat, Jack Handy's book up in Arbordale. There's others here. You owe twelve thousand, and you can't go to Jake for a loan. He's got a blind spot where gambling's concerned. He don't forbid his people from making a bet now and then, but he don't bail them out either. Tell me I'm wrong."

Midge shook his head. Mr. Wassermann had explained all this his first day. Midge hadn't known then that the new class of woman he'd be dating liked pretty much the same entertainments as the old.

"See, that's a problem. I spent more'n face value buying these up. I'm a reasonable man, though. I'll eat the difference. You got twelve grand, Midge?"

"You know I don't."

Little Angie smacked his face with the markers. Midge tool a step forward; so did Francis. Little Angie held up a finger, stopping them both. "Let's not be uncivil. There's a way you can work it off. You won't even have to pop a sweat."

Midge heard enough of the rest to understand. Mr. Wassermann, who had the ear of a number of important people, had promised to spoil an investment Little Angie wanted to make. The important people, he hinted, would be in a position to listen to reason if Mr. Wassermann were not available to counsel them otherwise. All Midge had to do to settle his debts was stand at his usual station outside the door to Mr. Wassermann's office the following morning and not leave it, no matter what he heard going on inside.

"What if I just owe you like I did the others?" Midge asked.

"They was getting impatient. If I didn't step in, you'd be wearing plaster instead of that flashy suit, peeing through a tube. And I got to tell you, patience ain't my what-you-call forte. Francis?"

The ugly bald wrestler produced a loop of stiff nylon fish-line from a pocket. Midge knew he could prevent Francis from making use of it, but there were others in Little Angie's employ who knew what a garrote was for. He couldn't fight them all. Sooner or later he'd run into a Sonny Rodriguez.

"I know what you're thinking," Little Angie said. There's always a place in my organization for a fellow knows the score. You won't be out of a job."

Midge hadn't been thinking about that at all. "Can I have time to think it over?"

"If I had time I'd wait for Jake to die of old age."

Midge agreed to the terms. Little Angie leered and tore up the markers. Francis looked disappointed as well as ugly.

The next morning outside Mr. Wassermann's office was as long a time as Midge had ever spent anywhere, including seven and a half rounds with Lincoln Flagg. Mr. Wassermann had some telephone calls to make and told him he'd be working through lunch, but that he'd make it up to him that night with the full twelve courses from Bon Maison, Midge's favorite restaurant back when I he was contending. He had an armchair for his personal use in the hallway, but today he couldn't stay seated in it more than three minutes at a stretch. He stood with his hands folded in front of him, then behind him, picked lint off the sleeve of his new gray gabardine, found imaginary lint on the crease of the trousers and picked that off too. He was perspiring heavily under his sixty-dollar shirt, despite what Little Angie had said; he, Midge, who used to work out with the heavy bag for an hour without breaking a sweat. This selling out was hard work.

Too hard, he decided, after twenty minutes. He would take his chances with Little Angle's threats. He rapped on the door, waited the customary length of time while he assumed Mr. Wassermann was calling for him to come in, then opened the door. The garrote didn't frighten him half as much as the antici-pation of the look of sadness on Mr. Wassermann's face when he told him about his part in Little Angie's plan.

Mr. Wassermann was not behind his desk. But he was.

When Midge leaned his big broken-knuckled hands on it and peered over the far edge, the first thing he saw was the tan soles of his employer's hand-lasted wingtips. Mr. Wassermann was still seated in his padded leather swivel, but the chair lay on its back. Mr. Wassermann's face was the same oxblood tint as his shoes and his tongue stuck out. Midge couldn't see the wire, but he'd heard it sank itself so deep in a man's neck it couldn't be removed without getting blood on yourself, so most killers didn't bother to try.

A torch lamp behind the desk had toppled over in the struggle and lay on the carpet, its bulb shattered. Both it and Mr. Wassermann must have made more than a little noise. The door that was usually concealed in the paneling to the left stood open. It was used by Mr. Wassermann's congressmen and the occasional other business associate who preferred not to be seen going in or coming out. It was one of the worst-kept secrets around town.

Midge felt sad. He walked around the desk, stepping carefully to avoid grinding bits of glass into the Brussels carpet, and looked down into his employer's bloodshot eyes.

"The thing is, Mr. Wassermann, I didn't really go into the tank."

Mr. Wassermann didn't say anything. But then Midge probably wouldn't have heard him If he had.

HOW'S MY DRIVING?

The truck stop was lit up like a Hollywood movie premiere, an oval of incandescence in an undeveloped landscape where a county road ducked under the interstate. I parked my rig in the football field-sized lot and went into the diner, a little unsteady on my pins. I'd been stuck for an hour in a snarl caused by someone's broken axle and a thousand cars slowing down to gape at it, and I'd hit the flask a few times to flatten my nerves. If I missed my contact tonight it would be another week before he came back the other direction.

Brooks and Dunn were whining on the retro-look juke as I took a stool at the end of the counter. Most of the other customers were seated in booths. I counted eleven, shoveling out their plates and blowing steam off their thick mugs. It was late and there was a lull between early escapees from the traffic jam and the next batch backed up at the scales. The waitress, a tired-looking blonde of forty or so, came over with a clean mug and a carafe. In those places they put coffee in front of you the way they do a glass of water in others.

I nodded at the question on her face and watched her pour. "I bet you hate these slow times," I said.

She was silent for a moment, looking at me, and I knew I was being sized up for a pickup artist or just friendly. "I don't know which is worse," she said then, "this or the rush. When it's on I need six hands to keep up, and when it isn't I don't know what to do with the two I've got."

"My old man said he'd rather work than wait." I sipped. She made a pretty good pot. There's a trick to brewing strong coffee without making it bitter.

"He a trucker too?"

"He was a hood. They've got him doing ninety-nine years and a day in Joliet for murder."

"Well, there's a conversation starter I don't hear every night."

But I could tell she didn't believe me.

I didn't try to set her straight. The whiskey had loosened me up too much. I needed to put something on top of it. "You serve breakfast all the time?"

She said sure, it's a truck stop, and I ordered scrambled eggs and a ham steak. She gave it to the cook through the pass-through to the kitchen without writing it down and left the counter to freshen the other customers' coffee. When she got back she served me and refilled my cup. She watched me eat.

"You seem pretty well adjusted for the son of a convict."

"I was grown when he went in," I said, chewing. "It wasn't his first time, though. He did two bits for manslaughter on plea deals. Cops figured him for at least fifteen, but they only got him good on the last one."

She hoisted her eyebrows. "He was a serial killer?"

"Hell, no. Serial killers are loonies who slept with their mothers. He was a pro."

"A hit man? Like for the mob?"

"Most of the time. Sometimes he freelanced, but you can get jammed up working for civilians. I wouldn't touch one of those."

I realized what I'd said and changed the subject in a hurry. "Got any more hash browns?"

She put in the order. A trucker came in, one of the sloppy ones with a belly and tobacco stains in the corners of his mouth, and sat down at the other end of the counter. She ordered him a burger and a Coke and came back with the hash browns. "You've got a real line of crap, but it's one I never heard. So how'd the cops trip him up?"

"Circumstantial evidence. He ran a bar in Jersey, and guys kept going in and never coming out. His lawyer objected, but the judge was a hard case and allowed it in. There was some other stuff, but the past history's what clinched it for the jury." I poured ketchup on the potatoes. "That was his mistake, always operating in the same place. The best way to avoid drawing suspicion is to move around a lot. One hit in Buffalo, the next in Kansas City, another in Seattle. Get yourself a front that involves plenty of travel."

"Like truck driving."

I took a long draught of coffee. I was going to have to change my brand of booze. The one I drank talked and talked. "Sure. Or sales. The bigger the territory, the less chance of the cops getting together and comparing notes. Anyway, that's how I'd do it."

"Trucking's better," she said. "No one looks twice. You all run to the same type."

I turned my head to look at Big Belly waiting for his hamburger. Then I grinned at her.

"Okay, two types. One looks like a pro wrestler gone to seed, the other like Randy Travis. The point is, there's a lot of both. Traveling salesmen are about extinct. You notice the ones that are left." She folded her arms and leaned them on the counter. There were circles under her eyes, and she was older than I liked them in general, but she had good cheekbones and a serious expression. I'd had my fill of the playful kind. "How do you work it? Do they call you, or do you check in?"

Just then the cook set the burger and a plate of slimy fries on the sill. She delivered them without comment and took up the same position at my end, arms folded on the counter.

I pushed away my plates, unrolled the pack from my sleeve, and held it up. A NO SMOKING sign hung in plain sight on the wall behind her, but she shrugged. I got out two, gave her one, and lit them both. "If I went in for that work," I said, blowing smoke, "I'd have them call that eight-hundred number on the back of my truck. You know the one."

She nodded. "'How's My Driving?' with the number to call and complain. I can't remember the last time I saw a truck that didn't have it."

"That's what's beautiful about it. I'd have it forwarded to my cell. If I cut someone off in traffic and he called, I'd tell him I'd look into it, blow him off, like I'm a dispatcher. The other kind, the paying kind, if the cops trace it I can always say it was a wrong number. If there were no complications I'd adjust my route and take care of business."

"Pretty smart."

"Smarter than my old man, anyway. Smart enough not to go in for that line of work."

She straightened up and put out her cigarette in what was left of my eggs. "I thought so. Just another pickup. The trouble with you guys is you've seen *Bonnie and Clyde* one too many times. You think every girl who slings hash is just waiting for her chance to hook up with some road-show Jesse James."

"*Badlands,* actually. But you've got me pegged."

She figured my bill, slapped it on the counter, and left to bus tables. I finished my cigarette and paid, leaving fifteen percent.

I wanted to leave more, but I'd done too much already to make her remember me. I went back out to my rig.

It's a nice one, a secondhand Freightliner with an orange tractor and a shiny silver trailer; when new it had set someone back the price of a house on the beach. In the sleeping quarters behind the seat I switched on the light, went over my notes one more time, and looked at the driver's license photo blowup and telephoto candids once again for luck, then fed them to the cross-shredder I'd added to the standard equipment. I looked at my watch. I had better than an hour to kill. His company had him on a tight schedule, and he couldn't afford to lose another job. The Feds had told him he had no more coming if he expected any more help from them.

Twenty to midnight. I took two more hits from the flask and went back into the diner.

Big Belly had finished his meal and left. I waited while she rang up a middle-aged tourist couple with fanny packs, then asked if she got off at midnight.

"Why? You going to buy me a cuppa and tell me you're an international spy?"

"I started off on the wrong foot. I'll make it cappuccino if it'll make up for being a jerk."

She thought that over. She frowned more attractively than most women smiled. I had an almost overpowering urge to see what her smile looked like. She was as hard to put away as the flask, which I had now in my hip pocket.

"I'm on till four," she said. "But I'm past due for a break. Coffee's fine, but I wouldn't mind a slice of pie."

She asked the cook to cover the counter and brought the coffees and a wedge of lemon meringue to a booth in the smoking section, away from the others. I produced the flask and when she nodded I trickled some from it into both cups. We tapped them together in an unspoken toast.

She made a face when she tasted it. "I suppose it's good whiskey, but you don't drink it in coffee for the taste, do you?"

"My old man only drank it this way when he had a cold."

"You're not going to talk about him again, are you?"

"That subject's closed."

We shared small talk, or what passed for it between strangers late at night. Her name was Elizabeth; she preferred Beth, but she had LIZ scripted on her uniform blouse and said I could call her that as long as she was dressed for this job. She was working two jobs to earn enough to pay a lawyer to get custody of her ten-year-old daughter. She was a recovering meth addict. Her lawyer said if she could stay clean another six months she had a better chance in court. "So much for budding romance," she said, forking pie into her mouth.

"If I go on hitting this stuff the way I've been lately, we'll both be in the same boat." I added more to my cup. She frowned again when I offered to freshen hers, then nodded. The coffee was still hot; the fumes entered my nose and speeded up the process. I had to close one eye to see only one of her.

"Conscience," she said. "I guess you have to anesthetize yourself to make a clean job of it."

I couldn't tell if she was needling me or if she was really interested. I asked her what her other job was.

"Not as glamorous as this. Tell me about some of the people you've killed."

I looked at her, closing one eye. Her mouth twitched at the corners. It was going to be one of those conversations. In the same vein I told her about Omaha and then Sioux Falls, that bitched-up job that had almost got me pinched. I'd spent a nervous day maneuvering myself back into position to make it good. I was careful to speak hypothetically, spinning a story to keep the lady's interest.

I put away the flask, but by then I wasn't paying as much attention as I should have. I told her what I was working on, an open contract; a hundred and fifty grand to the man who made an example of a mouthy errand boy who'd blabbed enough in court to take down a chunk of the East Coast and put himself in the Witness Protection Program. But Anderson was a grifter who couldn't resist the temptation to turn a dishonest dollar, even if it brought attention and he had to be relocated under yet another identity. At present he was delivering office furniture from Cincinnati to L.A. and back, with a new face courtesy of the taxpayers to keep him from being recognized in case of a chance encounter with a former acquaintance. I'd started out careful, but somewhere along the way I stopped being hypothetical and mentioned the fact that Anderson always put in at that truck stop and was due there in a little while.

"Do you use a gun?"

"I have, but it makes a lot of noise: A knife's better for close work, and you know right away if you made it good. Also it's cheaper to replace when you leave it at the scene, with the prints wiped off, and you don't get jammed up if the cops find one on you. A lot of truckers carry buck knives for quick repairs."

I heard myself then, and it sobered me in a hurry. Then she chuckled, shaking her head, and the smile turned out to have been worth waiting for.

"You sure do sling the bull." She finished her pie and slid away the plate. "I ought to dump my coffee in your lap. So why am I not doing that?"

I took out my pack and lit us both, relieved. "Maybe I'm the first guy you ever met in this place didn't think pushing a rig was the most romantic job in America. It's boring as hell is what it is. You make up stories just to keep from aiming straight at a bridge abutment."

"It's pretty clever, especially that bit about being able to move around being a big advantage. You ought to write for the movies."

"You need to know somebody," I said. "And it helps to know how to spell."

She laughed. I grinned. It was going to be all right. Then the cook made a racket behind the counter, and that meant her break was over. She thanked me for the pie and the entertainment, and I got up like a gentleman when she rose. She pressed against me briefly—probably an accident, but try telling that to my physical reaction. She switched her hips in the tight uniform walking away. I was going to have to stop in on my way back across country.

Back behind the wheel I stuck the flask in the glove compartment and fired up the diesel. The Anderson job was out, at least at that location. If I was to get a jump on all the others looking for a big payday I'd have to follow him when he left, run him off some lonely section of road, and do the job with a jack handle, or anything but a knife. It would help that he wasn't going by the name Anderson and that the Feds would make sure it didn't get out that a witness in their care came to a bad end. If Liz read about it, she'd think it was an accident and wouldn't connect it to me.

One thing was sure. I needed to save the whiskey from then on for after the job, as a treat instead of a stimulus to action.

Anderson pulled up half an hour late, his company rig plastered with mud from some detour down a dirt road, probably in search of a crap game. The man had no pride, in his workmanship or anything else. The cargo of Arrow shirts I was carrying may have been just a cover, but I'd deliver them on time. Apart from ridding the world of a rotten snitch, I'd be doing some dispatcher the favor of not having to can him.

He went into the diner, looking as sloppy as the way he approached his duties. I remembered what Liz had said about there being two types of trucker, the big-bellied kind and the kind that looked like Randy Travis. I adjusted the rearview for a look at the stalwart chin, the granite squint, the hair cut short at the temples and left long in front to tumble go-to-hell fashion over the forehead. She'd felt firm and warm pressing against me. I wanted another pull at the flask, but I tamped down the temptation with a smoke.

I dozed off, I think. I jumped, alert all at once and cursing, but Anderson's filthy tractor-trailer stood where he'd left it, and the clock on the dash told me only five minutes had passed. At least I'd had the presence of mind to ditch the butt in the ashtray, where it had smoked itself out. I didn't remember doing it. Blackouts are a good sign to cut back.

I turned on a late-night talk show for company: the war, the economy, yet another scandal on Capitol Hill. If I'd ever had reason to regret the path my life had taken, self-esteem was only a dial switch away. I put in Johnny Cash and tried to keep up with him on the *Rock Island Line.*

Forty minutes passed, an hour. I pictured Anderson lingering over a plate of slop, maybe chatting up Liz. I hoped to hell he wasn't trying to impress her with his career in crime.

I got restless after ninety minutes. His desks and crap were due in Milwaukee by noon. I didn't picture him highballing it to make his deadline. He was exceeding even the margin of ineptitude I'd drawn up for him. I ditched the cigarette I'd started and stepped down to investigate. He didn't know me from Donald Duck. I could sit slurping coffee on the stool next to his and he'd think I was just another gear-cruncher, feeling all superior because he was just slumming from the wise-guy life.

The place was jumping. Just in the time I'd been out of the

loop the lot had filled with Macks and Peterbilts and the odd Winnebago, and Liz was too busy filling cups and plunking down bowls of chili to notice me. There were more beer guts than Travises crowding the counter, but Anderson wasn't among them, nor at any of the booths, where the knights of the road sat belching onions and air-shifting down steep mountain grades for their bored audiences. I went down the narrow tiled corridor that led to the showers and toilets.

Anderson wasn't in any of them, not even the ladies' room, where a schnook like him might wander into without stopping to read the sign on the door. The only door left was marked EMPLOYEES ONLY.

He lay there on the floor among the mops and cartons of toilet paper and industrial-sized mustard dispensers, on his face in the middle of a stain that didn't look like anything but what it was. I bent to feel his neck for a pulse, but didn't get that far. The knife stuck out hilt-deep from just below his left shoulder blade, flat, with a brass heel and a printed wood grain on the steel handle. I groped for the buck knife in my left pants pocket, purely from reflex. It wasn't there.

The door flew open and the rest was shouting and shoving and my feet kicked out from under me and two hundred pounds of county law kneeling on my back and the muzzle of a big sidearm tickling the back of my neck. I heard my rights and felt my shoulders pulled almost out of their sockets and the cold, hard, heavy clamp of the cuffs on my wrists.

I kept my mouth shut, credit me that. I was as sober as a Shaker and met every pair of eyes that locked with mine during the hustle through the crowded diner and out the door toward the radio car, where some kind soul who cared whether I suffered a concussion pressed down my head with an iron palm, shoved me into the backseat, and slammed the door.

The lot was desert bright, sheriff's spotlights adding candle-power to the pole lamps, the night air throbbing with sirens grinding down and radios muttering and spectators' chatter and the monotonous drone of official voices ordering the crowd to disperse, go home to your families, nothing to see here. I sat staring at the gridded polyurethane sheet that separated me from the front seat, where a fullback in uniform sat on one haunch with a foot on the pavement, murmuring into a mike, lights twinkling on the Christmas-tree console that divided the bucket seats in front.

When I got tired of looking at that I stared at the carpeted floor at my feet. I hadn't a chance with a not-guilty plea. The cops would track me through the ICC log and place me at the scene of every hit I'd performed. A good prosecutor would find a way to bring that out in court, even if my knife in Anderson's back wasn't enough. ("Someone picked your pocket? That's your defense?") You can't argue with the record. I was pinned as tightly as my old man in his bar where customers kept going in and never came out.

I raised my eyes to meet those of the curious pressing in for a closer look before they were manhandled out of the way by the hard men who had taken over the truck stop. One of the pairs of eyes belonged to Liz, looking less tired now, with that smile on her face as she made a gun with her finger and shot me with it.

I didn't know what it meant at first. Our conversation had taken place on the other side of the flask and came drifting back in pieces. One piece slowed down long enough for me to reel in.

Her other job wasn't as glamorous as this.

And as she faded back into the crowd, I heard the rest, as clearly as if she were still speaking: "You don't have to move around. I see just as many opportunities as you do just staying in one place."

SATURDAY NIGHT AT THE MIKADO MASSAGE

The ironic thing about the night Mr. Ten Fifty-Five died on Iiko's table was that she was supposed to have that Saturday off.

She'd asked for the time three weeks in advance so she could spend the weekend with Uncle Trinh, who was coming to visit from Corpus Christi, Texas, where he worked on a shrimp boat, but the day before his bus left, he slipped on some fish scales and broke his leg. Now he needed money for doctors' bills, and Iiko had volunteered to work.

The Mikado Massage was located on Michigan Avenue in Detroit. On one side was an empty building that had once sheltered a travel agency. The Mystic Arts Bookshop was on the other and shared a common wall with the Mikado. There was a fire door in this wall, which came in handy during election years. When the mayor sent police with warrants, they invariably found the bookshop full of customers and the massage parlor empty. On the third Sunday of every month a man came to collect for the service of keeping the owner informed about these visits. Iiko had seen the man's picture under some printing on the side of a van with a loudspeaker on the roof. Detroit was the same as back home except for no Ho Chi Mirth on the billboards.

Although its display in the yellow pages advertised an all-Japanese staff, the Mikado's owner, Mr. Shigeta, was the only person in residence not Korean or Vietnamese, and he was never seen by the customers unless one of them became ungallant. He was a short, thick man of fifty-five or seventy with hair exactly like a seal's, who claimed to have stood in for Harold Sakata on the set of Goldfinger and had papered his little office with posters and lobby cards from the film. He kept a bottle of Polish vodka and a jar of pickled eggs in a crawlspace behind the radiator.

Iiko had been working there four months. She made less than the other masseuses because she was still on probation after a police visit to the Dragon's Gate in the suburb of Inkster, which had no fire door, and so she gave only massages, no specials. She kept track of the two months remaining on her sentence on a Philgas calendar inside her locker door.

The man she called Mr. Ten Fifty-Five always showed up at that time on Saturday night and always asked for Iiko. Because he reminded her a little of Uncle Trinh, she'd thought to do him a kindness and had explained to him, in her imperfect English, that he could get the same massage for much less at any hotel, but he said he preferred the Mikado. The hotels didn't offer Japanese music or heated floors or scented oils or a pink bulb in a table lamp with a paper kimono shade.

Normally, Saturday was the busiest night of the week, but this was the Saturday after Thanksgiving, when, as Mr. Shigeta explained, the customers remembered they were family men and stayed home. Mr. Ten Fifty-Five, therefore, was the only person she'd seen since early evening when Mr. Shigeta had gone home, leaving her in charge.

Mr. Ten Fifty-Five was duck-shaped and bald, with funny gray tufts that stood out on both sides of his head when he waddled in from the shower in a towel and sprawled face down on the table. He often fell asleep the moment she began to rub him down and didn't wake up even when she walked on his back, so it wasn't until she asked him to turn over that Iiko found out that this time he'd died.

Iiko recognized death. She'd been only a baby when the last American soldier left her village, but she remembered the marauding gangs that swept through after the Fall of Saigon, claiming to be hunting rebels but forcing themselves upon the women and carrying away tins of food and silver picture frames and setting the buildings on fire when they left. Iiko's brother Nguyen, sixteen years old, had tried to block the door of their parents' home, but one of the visitors stuck a bayonet between his ribs and planted a boot on his face to tug loose the blade. Iiko hung on to her mother's skirt during the walk to the cemetery. The skirt was white, the color of mourning in Vietnam, with a border of faded flowers at the hem.

When Iiko confirmed that Mr. Ten Fifty-Five's heart had stopped, she went through his clothes. This was much easier than picking pockets in Ho Chi Minh City, where one always ran the risk of being caught with one's hand in the pocket of another pickpocket. Iiko found car keys, a little plastic bottle two-thirds full of tiny white pills, a tattered billfold containing fifty-two dollars, and a folding knife with a stag handle and a blade that had been ground down to a quarter inch wide. She placed it and the money in the pocket of her smock and returned the clothes to the back of the chair. The tail of the shabby coat clunked when it flapped against a chair leg.

Iiko investigated. There was a lump at the bottom where the machine stitch that secured the lining had been replaced by a clumsy crosshatch of thread that didn't match the original. This came loose easily, and she removed a small green cloth sack with a drawstring, whose contents caught the pink light in seven spots of reflected purple. When she switched on the overhead bulb, the stones, irregular ovals the size of the charcoal bits she swept weekly from the brazier in the sauna, turned deep blue.

She found a place for the stones, then went out into the little reception area to call Mr. Shigeta at home. He would want to know that a customer had died so that when the police came they would find nothing of interest except a dead customer. While she was dialing, two men came in.

Both were Americans. One, a large black man with a face that was all jutting bones, wore jeans, a sweatshirt, and a Pistons jacket. He towered over his companion, a white man with small features and sandy hair done up elaborately, wearing a shiny black suit with a pinched waist and jagged lapels. Their eyes continued to move around the room after the men had come to a stop a few feet from the counter.

"Sorry, we close," Iiko said.

She was standing in front of the sign that said OPEN TILL MIDNIGHT.

"You're back open," said the sandy-haired man. "Long enough anyway to tell us where's the fat bald guy that came in here about eleven."

She shook her head, indicating that she didn't understand. It was not entirely a lie. The sandy-haired man, who did almost all the talking, spoke very fast.

"Come on, girlie, we know he's here. His car's outside."

"The stuff ain't in it, neither," said the black man.

"Shut up, Leon."

"Not know," said Iiko.

"Leon."

The black man put a hand inside his jacket and brought out a big silver gun with a twelve inch barrel. He pointed it at her and thumbed back the hammer.

The sandy man said, "Leon's killed three men and a woman, but he's never to my knowledge done a slant. Where's George?"

"Not know George," she said.

"Keep it on her. If she jumps, take off her head." The sandy man came around the counter.

Iiko stood still while the man ran his hands over her smock. She didn't even move when they lingered at her small breasts and crotch. He took the fifty-two dollars and the knife from her pockets. He showed Leon the knife.

"That's George's shank, all right," said the black man. "He carries it open when he has to walk more'n a block to his car. He's almost as scared of muggers as he is of guns."

The sandy man slapped Iiko's face. She remained unmoving. She could feel the hot imprint of his palm on her cheek.

"One more time before we disturb the peace, Dragon Lady. Where's George Myrtle?"

She turned and went through the door behind the counter. The two men followed.

In the massage room the sandy man felt behind Mr. Ten Fifty-Five's ear, then said, "Deader'n Old Yeller."

"I don't see no marks," Leon said.

"Of course not. Look at him. He as good as squiffed himself the day he topped two forty and started taking elevators instead of climbing the stairs. I bet he never said no to a second helping of mashed potatoes in his life. Check out his clothes."

Leon returned the big gun to a holster under his left arm and quickly turned out all the pockets of the coat and trousers, then with a grunt held the coat upside-down and showed his companion the place where the lining had been pulled loose.

The sandy man looked at Iiko. She saw something in his pale eyes that she remembered from the day her brother was killed.

"This ain't turning out the way I figured," the sandy man said. "I was looking forward to watching Leon bat around that tub of guts until he told us what he done with them hot rocks. I sure don't enjoy watching him do that to a woman. Especially not to a pretty little China doll like you. How's about sparing me that and telling me what you did with the merch?"

"Not know merch," she said truthfully.

Leon started toward her. The sandy man stopped him with a hand. He was still looking at Iiko.

"You got more of these rooms?" he asked.

After a moment she nodded and stepped in the direction of the curtain over the doorway. The black man's bulk blocked that path.

"Search the rest of the place, Leon. I'll take care of this."

"Sure?"

"Sure."

Leon went out. Iiko led the sandy man through the curtains and across the narrow hallway. This room was larger, although still small. A forest of bottles containing scented oils stood on a rack beside the massage table. The sandy man seized her arm and spun her around. They were close now, and the light in his eyes had changed. She could smell his aftershave, sticky and sharp.

"You're sure a nice little piece for a slant. I bet old George had some times with you. Especially at the end."

Iiko didn't struggle.

The sandy man said, "I could use a little rub myself. You rub me, I rub you. What do you say? Then we'll talk."

After a moment she nodded. "Take off clothes."

"You first."

He let go of her and stepped back, his small hard fists dangling at his sides. He watched her unbutton and peel off the smock. Without hesitating, she undid her halter top and stepped out of her shorts. She wore no underthings. She knew her body was good, firm and well-proportioned for her small frame. She could see in his eyes he approved.

He took a long breath and let it out. Then he took off his shiny black coat. He hung his suit carefully on the wooden hanger on the wall peg, folded his shirt and put it on the seat of the chair. His ribs showed, but his pale, naked arms and legs were sinewy, the limbs of a runner.

He saw that she saw. "I work out. I ain't going to do you no favor like George and clock out on the table."

She said nothing. He stretched out on his stomach on the padded table. "No oil," he said. "I don't want to ruin my clothes. Just powder."

She reached for the can of talcum. While her back was turned to him, she laid down the folding knife she had removed from the sandy man's pocket while he was holding her, poking it behind a row of bottles.

She sprinkled the powder on his back, set down the can, and worked her hands along his spine and scapula. His muscles jumped and twitched beneath her palms, not at all like the loose, unresisting flesh of Mr. Ten Fifty-Five. She had the impression the sandy man was poised to leap off the table at the first sign of suspicious behavior. She heard glass breaking in another part of the building as Leon continued his search for the blue stones.

Iiko was a good masseuse. Unlike some of her fellow employees, who merely went through the motions until the big moment when they asked the customers to turn over, Iiko had been trained by a licensed massage therapist. She flattered herself that she still managed to give satisfaction even under the strictures of probation. Gradually she felt the sandy man's body relax beneath her expert hands.

To maintain contact, she kept one palm on his lower spine while with the other she retrieved the knife from its hiding place on the rack of bottles, pried it open with her teeth, and with one swift underhand motion jammed the blade into his back as far as it would go and dragged it around his right kidney as if she were coring an apple. The sandy man made very little noise dying.

When the body had ceased to shudder, she dressed and left the room. The sound of a heavy piece of furniture scraping across a wooden floor told her that Leon was moving the desk in Mr. Shigeta's office. The way to the front door and out led directly past that room; she did not want to take the chance of running into the black man as he came out. She let herself into the Mystic Arts Bookshop by way of the fire door in the wall that separated the two establishments.

The shop had been closed for hours. She groped her way through darkness to the front door but found that exit barred by a deadbolt lock that required a key. The same was true of the back door. An ornamental grid sealed the windows. For a moment Iiko stood still and waited for her thoughts to settle. It would not be long before Leon discovered the sandy man's body, and then he would find the fire door. The lock was on the massage parlor side.

She switched on a light. Tall racks of musty-smelling books divided the room into narrow aisles. She removed a heavy dictionary from the reference section, carried it to the common wall, and set the book on the floor in front of the steel door. She repeated the procedure with another large book, and then another. At the end of ten minutes she had erected a formidable barrier. Then she sat down to catch her breath and wait.

She did not wait long. She jumped when the thumb latch went down, stood and backed away instinctively when the door moved a fraction of an inch and stopped, impeded by the stacked books. She had already located the telephone on a cluttered counter near the front door of the bookshop; now she lifted the receiver, dialed 911, and, when the operator came on, laid the receiver on its side facing the fire door.

Just then Leon pushed the door hard. Two of the stacks fell, creating an avalanche. Encouraged, the black man gave a lunge. More books tumbled, but now the pile was wedged tightly between the door and the first rack. It would not budge further.

Iiko switched off the light. A bank of deep shadow appeared on the side of the fire door nearest the latch, and she slipped into it noiselessly. The black man had worked up a sweat searching the Mikado for the missing stones. She could smell the clean sharp sting of it where she crouched.

Nothing stirred in the bookshop. She heard the black man's heavy breathing as he paused to gather his strength, heard the buzzing queries of the 911 operator coming through the earpiece of the telephone a dozen steps away.

With an explosive grunt, Leon threw all his weight against the door. The pile of books crumpled against the base of the rack. The rack teetered, tilted, hung at a twenty-degree angle for an impossible length of time; then it toppled. Books plummeted from its shelves. To the operator listening at police headquarters it must have sounded like an artillery barrage. Leon thrust his arm and shoulder through the widened opening. The big silver gun made the arm look ridiculously long. His entire body seemed to swell with the effort to squeeze past the edge of the door. He grunted again, and the noise turned into a howl of triumph as he stumbled into the bookshop.

But his eyes were not accustomed to the darkness, and he set his foot on a poorly balanced book that turned under his weight. He sprawled headlong across the pile.

The opening into the massage parlor was more than wide enough for Iiko. She darted through, and before Leon could get to his feet, she seized the door handle and yanked it shut behind her, flicking the lock button with her thumb.

In the next minute it didn't matter that the 911 operator could hear the black man pounding the steel door with his fists. The air was shrill with sirens, red and blue strobes throbbed through the windows of the Mikado. Gravel pelted the side of the building as the police cruisers skidded around the corner into the parking lot of the Mystic Arts.

Iiko did not pay much attention to the bullhorn-distorted demands for surrender next door, or even the rattle of gunfire when Leon, exhausted and confused by the turn of events since he and the sandy man had entered the Mikado, burst a lock and plunged out into the searchlights with the big silver gun in his hand. She was busy with the narrow metal dustpan she used to clean out the brazier in the sauna, sifting through the smoldering bits of charcoal in the bottom. The stones were covered with soot and difficult to distinguish from the coals, but when she washed them in the sink they shone with the same icy blueness that had caught her eye in the massage room.

The glowing coals had burned away the green cloth bag as she'd known they would. She wrapped the stones carefully in a flannel facecloth, put the bundle in the side pocket of the cloth coat she drew on over her smock, and started toward the front door. Then she remembered the fifty-two dollars the sandy man had taken from her and put in the pocket of his shiny black suit.

The sandy man was as she'd left him, naked and dead, only

paler than before. She thrust the money into her other side pocket and went out.

Waiting at the corner for the bus, Iiko thought she would take the stones to the pawnshop man who bought the jewelry and gold money clips she managed from time to time to take from the clothing of her customers. The pawnshop man knew many people and had always dealt with her honestly. She hoped the stones would sell for enough to settle some of Uncle Trinh's doctors' bills.

THE PIONEER STRAIN

"A rifle!" Vernon Thickett stared up at his fellow deputy from behind a steaming hot bowl of Maud Baxter's notorious Red River Chili and cursed.

Earl Briggs nodded. He was a lean country boy, leaner even than Thickett, and with his shock of unruly wheat-colored hair and freckle-spattered face he looked far too young to be wearing a star on his buff shirt. "That's what I said, Verne," he affirmed. "She's got a rifle and Lord knows how many cartridges up there and she threatened to blow a hole in her nephew's nice tailor-made suit if he didn't clear off her land."

"Did he take her advice?"

A quick grin flashed across the younger deputy's face. "You know Leroy, Verne. What do you think?"

"I think he took her advice. Where is he now?"

"Out on Route Forty-four. He called the office from one of those free telephones the Highway Department put in last spring."

"Madder'n a half-squashed bee, I expect." Thickett made a face at his untouched meal and pushed himself reluctantly to his feet. He towered over Earl by a full head. "Get in touch with Luke and Dan and tell 'em to get over to Molly's place on the double and wait for me.

No sirens—we don't want any state troopers in on this one. Then bring my car around in front of the office while I grab a gun. That's the only thing the old girl understands." When Earl had left to carry out his orders Thickett snatched a slice of bread from the table, spooned a quantity of chili onto it, slapped another slice on top of that, and, nodding to hefty Maud Baxter behind the counter, strode toward the door of the diner with the sandwich in his mouth.

He didn't say a word to Earl all the way out to Molly's place. Verne Thickett was not the law in Schuylerville, Oklahoma, but as long as Sheriff Willis was in the hospital recuperating from a gall bladder operation he was the next best thing. Until now his biggest headache had been the kids who kept stealing the outhouse from behind Guy Dawson's place and hauling it up onto the roof of whatever schoolteacher happened to be the target of their hostilities that week. As for Molly Dodd, she was trouble enough at any time, but the kind of trouble she usually caused seldom involved the law. Molly Dodd armed with a rifle was one problem he wouldn't wish on his worst enemy.

For the past two years she and her nephew, Leroy Cooper, had been engaged in a bitter legal battle with each other over the ownership of the 160 acres she lived on up in the Osage Hills. The Great Midwestern Bank and Trust Company, of which Leroy was the Schuylerville branch manager, claimed the land in lieu of payment on the loan it had made to Molly's late husband back in 1969, while she maintained that he had paid it off shortly before his death in 1973. Molly, now in her late seventies, had been part of Schuylerville for so long that most of the town had sided with her throughout the complex legal maneuvering, but that had come to an end three weeks before when the county court of appeals found in favor of the bank and issued an order for Molly Dodd's eviction.

Thickett berated himself for not having anticipated the present situation. The pioneer strain in Molly was too strong to allow her to give in easily. He remembered the story his father had told him of the time she had come home early from a visit to find the house dark and her best friend's flivver parked in the driveway. Instead of going in and shooting Clyde and his lover—which, according to the moral code of the time, would have seemed the natural thing to do—she had simply climbed into the shiny new car, driven it into the next county, and sold it. The story had it that Clyde ended the affair soon afterward, and there was no record in the sheriff's office of a car being stolen that year. True or not, the account was worthy of Molly's reputation for audacity and ingenuity. It was certainly a funnier story than the desperate one currently unfolding up in the hills.

Leroy Cooper's sedan was parked at the side of the private road that led to the house at the top of the hill. A pair of scout cars were parked across from it at different angles. Earl ground the car to a dusty halt behind the civilian vehicle and they got out.

Cooper separated himself from the two deputies with whom he had been conversing and came forward. "I want the woman arrested, Deputy!" he exclaimed shrilly. "Do you know she actually threatened to shoot me? I barely got out of there with my life!"

"Take it easy, Leroy." Thickett slid his Stetson to the back of his head with a casual movement of his right hand. "Do you mind telling me what you were doing up there in the first place?"

"I merely reminded her to vacate the premises before midnight tonight. That's the deadline set by the court. The bull-dozers come in tomorrow."

"That's our job, Leroy. Why didn't you call us first?"

The banker looked as if Thickett had just asked him to scrub out a spittoon with his monogrammed shirt. "This is a family matter, Deputy. There seemed no reason to involve the law."

"It's a little late for that, isn't it?—What've we got, Luke?"

Luke Madden, the older of the two deputies already on the scene, was a big man with a bulldog jaw and hair the color of dull steel. He had been a deputy when Wilbur Underhill stormed through the area in 1933, and his prized possession was a framed newspaper clipping which described his inconclusive shoot-out with the outlaw. He spoke with a Blue Diamond matchstick clamped between his teeth. "That cabin's bunted smack up against the side of the hill," he told Thickett. "There's only one way in or out by car, and this here's it. If you and Earl and Dan can keep her busy in front, Verne, I can sneak around the long way and take her from behind."

"How are you going to get in? Through the chimney?" The chief deputy squinted up at the gabled structure atop the hill. "I reckon we'll just go on up and give her the chance to surrender."

The four-car caravan took off with Earl and Thickett in the lead and Leroy Cooper timidly bringing up the rear in his gleaming sedan. They were rounding the final turn before the house when a shot rang out and a bullet starred the windshield between the two deputies in front. Earl yanked the wheel hard to the right. The unmarked cruiser jumped the bank and came to a jarring stop in a bed of weeds at the side of the road. They both spilled Out Thickett's side of the car and crouched there, guns drawn.

"Verne! Earl! You guys all right?" The voice was Luke Madden's, shouting from behind his car parked perpendicularly across the road. The way beyond it was completely blocked by the other two vehicles.

"We're fine!" Thickett shouted back. "Stay down!"

"She means business," said Earl. "Maybe I ought to radio the state troopers."

"No need. If Molly had meant to hit us, she would have hit us. I've seen her pick nails off a fence post at thirty yards. She's just trying to scare us."

"She's awful good at it."

No more shots accompanied the first one, and for a long time the only sound was that of an occasional breeze humming through the upper branches of the towering pines that surrounded the house on three sides. The dwelling itself appeared deserted. All but one of the tall front windows were shaded, the exception being the wide open one to the left of the front door. Five full minutes passed before a voice like a bull's bellow called out through the open window.

"You boys just get back into your automobiles and drive on out of here," it said. "I don't want to hurt nobody, but I will if I have to!"

Cupping his hands around his mouth, Thickett shouted, "Molly, this here's Vernon Thickett! Put down that rifle and let us come in! You're not a criminal! Don't act like one!"

There was a short silence. Then, from the house: "I've knowed you since you was a baby, Vernon, and you know I don't want to hurt you! But you know I will if it means keepin' what's mine!"

"That's what I want to talk to you about, Molly! I—" Vernon had started to rise when another shot sounded, the bullet zinging along the roof of the unmarked scout car, missing his right ear by a couple of inches. He dove to the ground. "I can see this is going to take more than just words," he said to Earl after a moment.

A series of six more reports followed in rapid succession, and Thicken turned his head as Luke Madden ran toward him in a crouch, bullets kicking up dirt at his heels. "Luke, what in hell do you think you're doing?" he demanded when the older deputy was sprawled beside him, panting heavily. "I thought I told you to stay put!"

"Look," said the other, once he'd caught his breath. "If I can get around to the other side of the hill without her seeing me, I can drop down onto the roof and climb in through one of those gabled windows. With you laying down a steady pattern of fire out here she won't suspect a thing until I grab her and take away the rifle."

"No! There's no telling what she'll do if you startle her! Go back. I'll call you when I need you."

"Verne—"

"You heard me! Get back there and help Dan keep an eye on Leroy in case he tries anything dumb."

The other muttered something unintelligible and sprinted back to his car as more shots sounded from the house.

Earl turned a pair of frank blue eyes on Vernon. "He might be right, you know. That may be the only way to get her out of there without bloodshed."

"Forget it," snapped Thickett. "The trouble with Luke Madden is he can't forget he's the one who almost got Wilbur Underhill. I'm not going to let him play hero at the expense of that frightened old woman."

"Have you got a better plan?"

Thickett thought. Suddenly he turned to his companion. "What's the name of that salesman from Tulsa, the one who retired and came here to live about five years ago? You know, the one Molly's sweet on?"

"Luther Briscoe?"

"Right. Ever since Clyde's death nobody's seen 'em apart, not even when she went to court. They do everything together.

There's that telephone down by the highway; get hold of him and see if you can get him up here. If anybody can talk her out of there, Briscoe can."

"I can't."

"Why not?"

"He left town yesterday to visit his sister in Kansas. He asked me to keep an eye on his house while he was gone. Said he wouldn't be back until Monday."

"Damn! Well, that just leaves Plan B." Thickett jammed his pistol into its holster and began unbuckling the belt.

"What are you doing?"

"I'm going in." He laid the gunbelt on the ground. "You're what?"

"I'm counting on our friendship to keep her from shooting me."

"Now who's playing hero? You can't be sure of—"

"Hold your fire, Molly!" Thickett shouted through cupped hands. "I'm coming in and I'm unarmed!"

"Don't, Vernon!" The answering bellow held a desperate edge. "I mean what I say! I'll scatter your brains all over these hills!"

"I don't think you will, Molly." Slowly he rose to his feet. A bullet spanged against the roof of the scout car.

Thickett signaled the other deputies to hold their fire and stepped clear of the car. He could see Molly's rifle barrel pointing through the window. Cautiously he took a step forward.

The second shot snatched his hat off his head. He hesitated, then moved on. A third slug whined past his left ear but he kept walking. The next three shots were snapped off so rapidly they sounded as if they had come from a machine-gun. They struck the ground at his feet and spat gravel onto his pantlegs. By this time he was almost to the door. Two more steps and he was inside, where he closed the door behind him.

It was a moment before his eyes adjusted themselves to the dim light inside the house. When they had, his first thought was that the interior had not changed since he was a boy. The Victorian clutter, from the overstuffed rockers festooned with doilies to the glass-fronted china cabinets and papered walls upon which hung framed and faded prints of every conceivable shape and size, was the same as he remembered it. The only difference was the pile of cartridges on the pedestal table beside the door. Beyond it, Molly Dodd stood in the shadows at the open front window, her dark eyes glittering above the stock of the 30-year-old carbine she held braced against her shoulders. Thickett was looking right down its bore.

"Say your piece and get out." Her voice was taut. Small but wiry, she wore her black hair pulled straight back into a tight bun. Although her eyes were small above her hooked nose, they had a remarkable depth of expression. Her mouth was wide and turned down at the corners in a permanent scowl. Her print dress looked new, as did the sweater she wore buttoned at the neck like a cape. The firearm remained steady in her hands.

"Why don't you give me the gun, Molly?" Vernon asked quietly. "You aren't going to shoot anyone."

"When it comes to protectin' my property I'd shoot my own son if I had one," she snapped.

"You want to tell me about it?"

There was an almost indiscernible change in the expression of her eyes. "This place is mine," she said. "I know what the courts said, but they was wrong. They didn't see the record that proved Clyde paid off that loan because it don't exist no more. Not after that slippery nephew of mine got rid of it."

"Why would Leroy do that?" Thickett began to breathe a little more easily. He had her talking now.

"Why do you think? He knows there's oil on this land just like everybody else. If he can grab it for his bank he'll make hisself a big man and maybe they'll forget about checkin' his books like they been threatenin'."

"His books?"

She nodded curtly. Her eyes were black diamonds behind the peepsight of the rifle. "He's been stealin' money from his accounts for years. You seen that car he drives, the clothes he wears. He can't afford them on his salary. I was in the bank once and overheard a man threatenin' to take his books to the main branch in Oklahorna City to have 'em checked out. Leroy fell all over hisself tryin' to talk him out of it."

Thickett found himself growing interested in spite of the situation. "You say he destroyed the record that proved Clyde repaid the loan? Don't you have any proof of your own? What about a receipt?"

"Clyde never told me what he done with it. I been all over the house. It ain't here."

"What did you hope to gain by barricading yourself in the house?"

She smiled then, a bitter upturn of her cracked and pleated lips. "I wanted to see that squirrel's face when I stuck this here carbine under his nose. I never meant to drag you boys into it, Vernon."

"Don't you think it's gone far enough? Come on, Molly. We're old friends. Give me the piece."

She hesitated. Slowly the hard glitter faded from her eyes. Now she was just a tired old woman. At length she lowered the rifle and handed it to him.

Now that the danger was over, the deputy felt no triumph. For a long moment he regarded Molly with compassionate eyes. "What are your plans?" he asked.

"I sent my luggage on to Mexico this morning."

"Mexico? Why Mexico?"

"That's where Clyde and me spent our honeymoon. I got a reservation on a plane leavin' tonight from Tulsa. Don't suppose I'll make it now."

"Not if Leroy decides to press charges."

"That squirrel? Don't worry, he won't do nothin' that might attract attention." She looked at him apologetically. "I sure am sorry about that busted windshield."

He laughed good-naturedly. "You're good for it, Molly. Besides, the experience was almost worth it."

There was an embarrassed silence. Then: "What about Luther Briscoe? What was he going to think when he got back from Kansas and found you gone?"

"That's his business, I expect."

Thickett chose not to press the point. "Well," he drawled, "I'm faced with a decision. I can either put you in jail or drive you into Tulsa in time to catch your plane. Since my duty is to the citizens of Schuylerville, I think I'd be acting in their best interests if I saved them the expense of your room and board and took you into Tulsa."

She placed an affectionate hand on his arm. "You're a good boy, Vernon. I always said that."

It was dusk when Thickett eased the scout car he had borrowed from Luke Madden into the parking slot in front of the sheriff's office and went in. After the long drive back from Tulsa, it felt good to be using his legs again.

Earl Briggs, on his feet behind Thickett's desk, was hanging up the telephone as the chief deputy entered.

"I'm glad you're still here, Earl," Thickett said. "First thing tomorrow morning I want you to get in touch with the Great Midwestern Bank and Trust Company in Oklahoma City and—what is it?"

The look on the boy's face sent a wave of electricity through Thickett's weary limbs.

"That was Leroy Cooper," said Earl, inclining his head toward the telephone. "He just got back to find his head cashier tied up and gagged and the rest of his employees locked in the vault. Seems the bank was held up for a quarter of a million dollars while we were all out at Molly's place. You'll never guess who he says did it."

Thickett felt a sinking sensation as the pieces fell into place. He tightened his grip on the doorknob. "Luther Briscoe."

Earl stared at him. "How on earth did you know that?" he said.

THE USED

"But I never been to Iowa!" Murch protested.

His visitor sighed. "Of course not. No one has. That's why we're sending you there."

Slouched in the worn leather armchair in the office Murch kept at home, Adamson looked more like a high school basketball player than a federal agent. He had baby-fat features without a breath of whisker and collar-length sandy hair and wore faded Levi's with a tweed jacket too short in the sleeves and a paisley tie at three-quarter mast. His voice was changing, for God's sake. The slight bulge under his left arm might have been a sandwich from home.

Murch paced, coming to a stop at the basement window. His lawn needed mowing. The thought of it awakened the bursitis in his right shoulder. "What'll I do there? Don't they raise wheat or something like that? What's a wheat farmer need with a bookkeeper?"

"You won't be a bookkeeper. I explained all this before." The agent sat up, resting his forearms on his bony knees. "In return for your testimony regarding illegal contributions made by your employer to the campaigns of Congressmen Disdale and Reicher and Senator Van Horn, the Justice Department promises immunity from prosecution. You will also be provided with protection during the trial, and afterwards a new identity and relocation to Iowa. When you get there, you'll find a job waiting for you selling hardware, courtesy of Uncle Sam."

"What do I know about hardware? My business is with numbers."

"An accounting position seemed inadvisable on the off chance Redman's people traced you west. They'd never think of looking for you behind a sales counter."

"You said he wouldn't be able to trace me!" Murch swung around.

Adamson's lips pursed, lending him the appearance of a teenage Cupid. "I won't lie and say it hasn't happened. But in those cases there were big syndicate operations involved, with plenty of capital to spend. Jules Redman is light cargo by comparison. It's the senator and the congressmen we want, but we have to knock him down to get to them."

"What's the matter, they turn you down?"

The agent looked at him blankly.

Murch had to smile. "Come on, I ain't been in this line eighteen years I don't see how it jerks. Maybe these guys giving your agency a hard time on appropriations, or—" He broke off, his face brightening further. "Say, didn't I read where this Van Horn is asking for an investigation into clandestine operations? Yeah, and maybe the others support him. So you sniff around till something stinks and then tell them if they play ball you'll scratch sand over it. Only they don't feel like playing, so now you go for the jugular. Am I close?"

"I'm just a field operator, Mr. Murch. I leave politics to politicians." But the grudging respect in the agent's tone was enlightening.

"What happens if I decide not to testify?"

"Then you'll be wearing your numbers on your shirt. For three counts of conspiracy to bribe a member of the United States Congress."

They were watching each other when the doorbell rang upstairs. Murch jumped.

"That'll be your escort," Adamson suggested. "I've arranged for a room at a motel in the suburbs. The local police are lending a couple of plainclothesman to stay there with you until the trial Monday. It's up to you whether I ask them to take you to jail instead."

"One room?" The bookkeeper's lip curled.

"There's an economy move on in Washington." Adamson got out of the chair and stood waiting. The doorbell sounded again.

"I want a color TV in the room," said Murch. "Tell your boss no color TV, no deal."

The agent didn't smile. "I'll tell him." He went up to answer the door.

He shared a frame bungalow at the motel between the railroad and the river with a detective sergeant named Kirdy and his relief, a lean, chinless officer who watched football all day with the sound turned down. He held a transistor radio in his lap; it was tuned in to the races. Kirdy looked smaller than he was. Though his head barely reached the bridge of Murch's nose, he took a size forty-six jacket and had to turn sideways to clear his shoulders through doorways. He had kind eyes set incongruously in a slab of granite. No-Chin never spoke except to warn his charge away from the windows. Kirdy's conversation centered around his grand-daughter, a blonde tyke of whom he had a wallet full of photos.

The bathroom was heated only intermittently by an electric baseboard unit and the building shuddered whenever a train went past. But Murch had his color TV.

At half past ten Monday morning, he was escorted into the court by Adamson and another agent who looked like a rock musician. Jules Redman sat at the defense table with his attorney. Murch's employer was small and dark, with an old-time gunfighter's handlebar mustache and glossy black hair combed over a bald spot. Their gazes met while the bookkeeper was being sworn in, and from then until recess was called at noon Redman's tan eyes remained on the man in the witness chair.

Charles Anthony Murch—his full name felt strange on his tongue when the court officer asked him for it—was on the stand two days. His testimony was complicated, having to do with dates and transactions made through dummy corporations, and he consulted his notebook often while the jurors stifled yawns and the spectators fidgeted and inspected their fingernails. After adjournment the first day, the witness was whisked along a circuitous route to a hotel near the airport, where Kirdy and his partner awaited their duty. On the way Adamson was talkative and in good spirits. Already he spoke of how his agency would proceed against the congressmen and Senator Van Horn after Redman was convicted. Murch was silent, remembering his employer's eyes.

The defense attorney, white-haired and grandfatherly behind a pair of half-glasses, kept his seat during cross-examination the next morning, reading from a computer printout sheet on the table in front of him while the government's case slowly fell to pieces. Murch had thought that his dismissal from that contracting firm up state was off the books, and he was surprised to learn that someone had penetrated his double-entry system at the insurance company he had left in Chicago. Based on this record, the lawyer accused the bookkeeper of entering the so-called campaign donations into Redman's ledger to cover his own thefts. The jurors' faces were unreadable, but as the imputation continued Murch saw the corners of the defendant's mustache rise slightly and watched Adamson's eyes growing dull.

The jury was out twenty-two hours, a state record for that kind of case. Jules Redman was found guilty of resisting arrest, reduced from assaulting a police officer (he had lost his temper and knocked down a detective during an unsuccessful search of his office for evidence), and was acquitted on three counts of bribery. He was fined a hundred dollars.

Adamson was out the door on the reporters' scurrying heels. Murch hurried to catch up.

"You just don't live right, Charlie."

The bookkeeper held up at the hissed comment. Redman's diminutive frame slid past him in the aisle and was swallowed up by a crowd of well-wishers gathered near the door.

The agent kept a twelve-by-ten cubicle in the federal building two floors up from the courtroom where Redman had been set free. When Murch burst in, Adamson was slumped behind a gray steel desk deep in conversation with his rock musician partner.

"We had a deal," corrected the agent, after Murch's panicky interruption. His colleague stood by brushing his long hair out of his eyes. "It was made in good faith. We gave you a chance to volunteer any information from your past that might put our case in jeopardy. You didn't take advantage of it, and now we're all treading water in the toilet."

"How was I to know they was gonna dig up that stuff about those other two jobs? You investigated me. You didn't find nothing." The ex-witness's hands made wet marks on the desk top.

"Our methods aren't Redman's. It takes longer to subpoena personnel files than it does to screw a magnum into a clerk's ear and say gimme. Now I know why he didn't try to take you out before the trial." He paused. "Is there anything else?"

"Damn right there's something else! You promised me Iowa, win or lose."

Adamson reached inside his jacket and extracted a long narrow folder like the airlines use to put tickets in. Murch's heart leaped. He was reaching for the folder when the agent tore it in half. He put the pieces together and tore them again. Again, and then he let the bits flutter to the desk.

For a numb moment the bookkeeper goggled at the scraps. Then he lunged, grasping Adamson's lapels in both hands and lifting. "Redman's a killer!" He shook him. The agent clawed at his wrists, but Murch's fingers were strong from their years spent cramped around pencils and the handles of adding machines. Adamson's right hand went for his underarm holster, but his partner had gotten Murch in a bear hug and pulled. The front of the captive agent's coat tore away in his hands.

Adamson's chest heaved. He gestured with his revolver. "Get him the hell out of here," His voice cracked.

Murch struggled, but his right arm was yanked behind him and twisted. Pain shot through his shoulder. He went along, whimpering. Shoved out into the corridor, he had to run to catch his balance and slammed into the opposite wall, knocking a memo off a bulletin board. The door exploded shut.

A group of well-dressed men standing nearby stopped talking to look at him. He realized that he was still holding pieces of Adamson's jacket. He let them fall, brushed back his thinning hair with a shaky hand, adjusted his suit, and moved off down the corridor.

Redman and his lawyer were being interviewed on the

courthouse steps by a television crew. Murch gave them a wide berth on his way down. He overheard Redman telling the reporters he was leaving tomorrow morning for a week's vacation in Jamaica. Ice formed in the bookkeeper's stomach. Redman was giving himself an alibi for when Murch's body turned up.

Anyway, he had eighteen hours' grace. He decided to write off the stuff he had left back at the hotel and took a cab to his house on the west side. For years he had kept two thousand dollars in cash there in case he needed a getaway stake in a hurry. By the time he had his key in the front door lock he was already breathing easier; Redman's men wouldn't try anything until their boss was out of the country, and a couple of grand could get a man a long way in eighteen hours.

His house had been ransacked.

They had overlooked nothing. They had torn up the rugs, pulled apart the sofa and easy chairs and slit open the cushions, taken pictures down from the wall and dismantled the frames, removed the back panel from the TV set, dumped out the flour and sugar canisters in the kitchen. Even the plates had been unscrewed from the wall switches. The orange juice can in which he had kept the rolled bills in the freezer compartment of the refrigerator lay empty on the linoleum.

The sheer cold logic of the operation dizzied Murch.

Even after they had found the money they had gone on to make sure there were no other caches. His office alone, its contents smeared out into the passage that led to the stairs, would have taken hours to reduce to its present condition. The search had to have started well before the verdict was in, perhaps even as early as the weekend he had spent in that motel by the railroad tracks. Redman had been so confident of victory he had moved to cut off the bookkeeper's escape while the trial was still in progress.

He couldn't stay there. Probably he was already being

watched, and the longer he remained the greater his chances of being kept prisoner in his own home until the word came down to eliminate him. He stepped outside. The street was quiet except for some noisy kids playing basketball in a neighbor's driveway and the snort of a power mower farther down the block. He started walking toward the corner.

Toward the bank. They'd taken his passbook, too, but he had better than six thousand in his account and he could borrow against that. Buy a used car or hop a plane. Maybe even go to Jamaica, stretch out on the beach next to Redman, and wait for his reaction. He smiled at that. Confidence warmed him, like whiskey in a cold belly. He mounted the bank steps, grasped the handle on the glass door. And froze.

He was alerted by the one reading a bank pamphlet in a chair near the door. There were no lines at the tellers' cages and no reason to wait. He spotted the other standing at the writing table, pretending to be making out a deposit slip. Their eyes wandered the lobby from time to time, casually. Murch didn't recognize their faces, but he knew the type: early thirties, jackets tailored to avoid telltale bulges. He reversed directions, moving slowly to keep from drawing attention. His heart started up again when he cleared the plate glass.

It was quarter to five, too late to reach another branch before closing, and even if he did he knew what would be waiting for him. He knew they had no intention of molesting him unless he tried to borrow money. They were running him like hounds, keeping him within range while they waited for the go-ahead. He was on a short tether with Redman on the other end.

But a man who juggled figures the way Murch did had more angles than the Pentagon. He hailed a cruising cab and gave the driver Bart Morgan's address on Whitaker.

*　*　*

Morgan's Laundromat was twice as big as the room in back where the real business was conducted, with a narrow office between to prevent the ringing of the telephones from reaching the housewives washing their husbands' socks out front. Murch found the proprietor there counting change at the card table he used for a desk. Muscular but running to fat, Morgan had crew cut steel-gray hair and wore horn-rimmed glasses with a hearing aid built into one bow. His head grew straight out of his T-shirt.

"How they running, Bart?"

"They need fixing." He reached across the stacked coins to shake Murch's hand.

"I meant the horses, not the machines."

"So did I."

They laughed. When they were through, Murch said, "I need money, Bart."

"I figured that." The proprietor's eyes dropped to the table. "You caught me short, Charlie. I got bit hard at the Downs Saturday."

"I don't need much, just enough to get out of the city."

"I'm strapped. I wish to hell I wasn't but I am." He took a quarter from one stack and placed it atop another. "You know I'd do it if I could."

The bookkeeper seized his wrist gently. "You owe me, Bart If I didn't lend you four big ones when the Dodgers took the Series, you'd be part of an off-ramp somewhere by now."

"I paid back every cent."

"It ain't the money, it's doing what's needed."

Morgan avoided his friend's eyes.

"Redman's goons been here, ain't they?"

Their gazes met for an instant, then Morgan's dropped again. "I got a wife and a kid that can't stay out of trouble." He spoke quietly. "What they gonna do I don't come home some night, or the next or the next?"

"You and me are friends."

"You got no right to say that." The proprietor's face grew red, "You got no right to come in here and ask me to put my chin on the block."

Murch tightened his grip. "If you don't give it to me I'll take it,"

"I don't think so." Morgan leaned backs exposing a curved black rubber grip pressing into his paunch above the waistband of his pants.

Murch said, "You'd do Redman's job for him?"

"I'll do what I got to to live, same as you."

Telephones jangled in back, all but drowned out by the whooshing of the machines Out front. The bookkeeper cast away his friend's wrist. "Tell your wife and kid Charlie said goodbye." He went out, leaving the door open behind him.

"You got no right, Charlie."

Murch kept going. Morgan stood up, shouting to be heard over the racket of the front-loaders. "You should of come to me before you went running to the feds! I'd of give you the odds!"

His visitor was on the street.

Dusk was gathering when he left the home of his fourth and last friend in the city. His afflicted shoulder, inflamed by the humid weather and the rough treatment he had received at Adamson's office, throbbed like an aching tooth. His hands were empty. Like Bart Morgan, Gordy Sharp and Ed Zimmer pleaded temporary poverty, Zimmer stepping out onto the porch to talk while his family remained inside. There was no answer at Henry Arbogast's, yet Murch swore he had seen a light go off in one of the windows on his way up the walk.

Which left Liz.

He counted the money in his wallet. Forty-two dollars. He had spent almost thirty on cabs, leaving himself with just enough for a room for the night if he failed to get shed of the city. Liz was living in the old place two miles uptown. He sighed, put away the billfold, and planted the first sore foot on concrete.

Night crept out of the shadowed alleys to crouch beyond the pale rings cast by the street lights. He avoided them, taking his comfort in the invisibility darkness lent him. Twice he halted, breathing shallowly, when cars crawled along the curb going in his direction, then he resumed walking as they turned down side streets and picked up speed. His imagination flourished in the absence of light.

The soles of his feet were sending sharp pains splintering up through his ankles by the time he reached the brickfront apartment house and mounted the well-worn stairs to the fourth floor. Outside 4C he leaned against the wall while his breathing slowed and his face cooled. Straightening, he raised his fist, paused, and knocked gently.

A steel chain prevented the door from opening beyond the width of her face. Her features were dark against the light behind her, sharper than before, the skin creased under her eyes and at the corners of her mouth. Her black hair was streaked in mouse-color and needed combing. She had aged considerably.

"I knew you'd show up," she snapped, cutting his greeting in half. "I heard all about the verdict on the six o'clock news. You want money."

"I'm lonesome, Liz. I just want to talk." He'd forgotten how quick she was. But he had always been able to soften her up in the past.

"You never talked all the time we was married unless you

wanted something. I can't help you, Charlie." She started to close the door.

He leaned on it. His bad shoulder howled in outrage.

"Liz, you're my last stop. They got all the other holes plugged." He told her about Adamson's broken promise, about the bank and his friends. "Redman'll kill me just to make an example."

She said, "And you're surprised?"

"What's that supposed to mean?" He controlled his anger with an effort. That had always been her chief weapon, her instinct for the raw nerve.

"There's two kinds in this world, the ones that use and the ones that get used." Her face was completely in shadow now, unreadable. "Guys like Redman and Adamson squeeze all the good out of guys like you and then throw you away. That's the real reason I divorced you, Charlie. You was headed for the junkpile the day you was born. I just didn't want to be there to see it."

"Christ, Liz, I'm talking about my life!"

"Me too. Just a second." She withdrew, leaving the door open.

He felt the old warmth returning. Same old Liz: Deliver a lecture, then turn around and come through after all. It was like enduring the sermon at the Perpetual Mission in return for a hot meal and roof for the night.

"Here." Returning, she thrust a fistful of something through the opening. He reached for it eagerly. His fingers closed on cold steel.

He recoiled, tried to give back the object, but she'd dropped her hand. "You nuts?" he demanded. "I ain't fired a gun since the army!"

"It's all I got to give you. Don't let them find out where it came from."

"What good is it against a dozen men with guns?"

"No good, the way you're thinking. I wait tables in Redman's neighborhood, I hear things. He likes blowtorches. Don't let them burn you alive, Charlie."

He was still staring, holding the .38 revolver like a handful of popcorn, when she shut the door. The lock snapped with a noise like jaws closing.

It was a clear night. The Budweiser sign in the window of the corner bar might have been cut with an engraving tool out of orange neon. Someone gasped when he emerged from the apartment building. A woman in evening dress hurried past on a man's arm, her face tight and pale in the light coming out through the glass door, one brown eye rolling back at Murch. He'd forgotten about the gun. He put it away.

His subsequent pounding had failed to get Liz to open her door. If he'd wanted a weapon he'd have gotten it himself; the city bristled with unregistered iron. He fingered the unfamiliar thing in his pocket, wondering where to go next. His eyes came to the bright sign in the bar window.

Blood surged in his ears. Murch's robberies had all been from company treasuries, not people, his weapons figures in ledgers. Demanding money for lives required a steady hand and the will to carry out the threat. It was too raw for him, too much like crime. He started walking away from the bar. His footsteps slowed halfway down the block and stopped twenty feet short of the opposite corner. The pedestrian signal changed twice while he was standing there. He turned around and retraced his steps. He was squeezing the concealed revolver so hard his knuckles ached.

The establishment was quiet for that time of the evening, deserted but for a young bartender in a red apron standing at the cash register. The jukebox was silent. As Murch approached, the employee turned unnaturally bright eyes on him. The light from the beer advertisement reflecting off the bar's cherrywood finish flushed the young man's face. "Sorry, friend, we're—"

Murch aimed the .38. His hand shook.

The bartender smiled weakly.

"This ain't no joke! Get 'em up!" He tried to make his voice tough. It came out high and ragged.

Slowly the young man raised his hands. He was still smiling. "You're out of luck, friend."

Murch told him to shut up and open the cash register drawer. He obeyed. It was empty.

"Someone beat you to it," explained the bartender. "Two guys with shotguns came in an hour ago, shook down the customers, and cleaned me out. Didn't even leave enough to open up with in the morning. You just missed the cops."

His smile burned. Murch's finger tightened on the trigger and the expression was gone. The bookkeeper backed away, bumped into a table. The gun almost went off. He turned and stumbled toward the door. He tugged at the handle; it didn't budge. The sign said PUSH. He shoved his way through to the street. Inside, the bartender was dialing the telephone.

The night air stung Murch's face, and he realized there were tears on his cheeks. His thoughts fluttered wildly. He caught them and sorted them into piles with the discipline of one trained to work with assets and debits. Redman couldn't have known he would pick this particular place to rob, even had he suspected the bookkeeper's desperation would make him choose that course. Blind luck had decided whom to favor, and as usual it wasn't Charlie Murch.

A distant siren awakened him to practicalities. soon he would be a fugitive from the law as well as from Redman; he wasn't cold enough to go back and kill the bartender to keep him from giving the police his description. He pocketed the gun and ran.

His breath was sawing in his throat two blocks later when he spotted a cab stopped at a light. He sprinted across to it, tore open the back door, and threw himself into a seat riddled with cigarette burns.

"Off duty, bub," announced the driver, hanging a puffy, stubbled face over the back of his seat. "Oil light's on. I'm on my way back to the garage to see what's wrong."

There was no protective panel between the seats. His passenger thrust the handgun in his face and thumbed back the hammer.

The driver sighed heavily. "All I got's twelve bucks and change. I ain't picked up a fare yet."

He was probably lying, but the light was green and Murch didn't want to be arrested arguing with a cabbie. "Just drive."

They passed a prowl car on its way toward the bar, its siren gulping, its lights flashing. Murch fought the urge to duck, hiding the gun instead. The county lock-up was full of men who would ice him just to get in good with Redman.

He got an idea that frightened him. He tried pushing it away, but it kept coming back.

"Mister, my engine's overheating."

Murch glanced up. The cab was making clunking noises. The warning light on the dash glowed angry red. They had gone nine blocks. "All right, pull over." The driver spun the wheel. As he rolled to a stop next to the curb the motor coughed, shuddered, and died. Steam rolled out from under the hood.

"Start counting." The passenger reached across the front seat and tore the microphone free of the two-way radio. "Don't get out till you reach a thousand. If you do, you won't have time to be sorry you did. You'll be dead." He slid out and slammed the door on six.

He caught another cab four blocks over, this time without having to use force. It was a twenty-dollar ride out to the posh residential district where Jules Redman lived. He tipped the cabbie five dollars. He had no more use for money.

The house was a brick ranch-style in a quiet cul-de-sac studded with shade trees. Murch found the hike to the front door effortless; for the first time in hours he was without pain. On the step he took a deep breath, let half of it out, and rang the bell. He took out the gun. Waited.

After a lifetime the door was opened by a very tall young man in a tan jacket custom-made to contain his enormous chest. It was Randolph, Redman's favorite bodyguard. His eyes flickered when he recognized the visitor. A hand darted inside his jacket.

The reports were very loud. Murch fired a split-second ahead of Randolph, shattering his sternum and throwing off his aim so that the second bullet entered the bookkeeper's left thigh. He had never been shot before; it was oddly sensationless, like the first time he had had sex. The bodyguard crumpled.

Murch stepped across him. He could feel the hot blood on his leg, nothing else. Just then Redman appeared in an open doorway beyond the staircase. When he saw Murch he froze. He was wearing a maroon velour robe over pajamas and his feet were in slippers.

The bookkeeper was motionless as well. What now? He hadn't expected to get this far. He had shot Randolph in self-defense; he couldn't kill a man in cold blood, not even this one, not even when that was the fate he had planned for Murch.

Redman understood. He smiled under his mustache. "Like I said before, Charlie, you just don't live right."

Another large man came steadily through a side door, towed by an automatic pistol. He was older than Randolph and wore neither jacket nor necktie, his empty underarm holster exposed. This was the other bodyguard. He held up before the sight that met his eyes.

"Kill him, Ted," Redman said calmly.

Murch's bullet splintered one of the steps in the staircase. He'd aimed at the banister, but that was close enough. "Next one goes between your boss's eyes," he informed the bodyguard.

Ted laid his gun on the floor and backed away from it, raising his hands.

The bookkeeper felt no triumph. He wondered if it was fear that was making him numb or if he just didn't care. To Redman: "Over here."

Redman hesitated. Murch cocked the revolver. The racketeer approached cautiously.

"Pick that up." Murch indicated Randolph's gun lying where he had dropped it when he fell. "Slow," he added, as Redman stooped to obey.

He accepted the firearm between the thumb and forefinger of his free hand and dropped it carefully into a pocket to avoid smearing the fingerprints. To Ted: "Get the car."

Murch was waiting in front with his hostage when the bodyguard drove the Cadillac out of the garage. "Okay, get out," he told Ted.

He made Redman get behind the wheel and climbed in on the passenger's side. "Start driving. I'll tell you what turns to make." He spoke through clenched teeth. His leg was starting to ache and he was feeling light-headed from the blood loss.

The bodyguard watched them until they reached the end of the driveway. Then he swung around and sprinted back inside.

"He'll be on the phone to the others in two seconds," jeered Redman. "How far you think you'll get before you bleed out?"

"Turn right," Murch directed.

The big car took the bumps well. Even so, each one was like a red-hot knife in the bookkeeper's thigh. He made himself as comfortable as possible without taking his eyes off the driver, the revolver resting in his lap with his hand on the butt. He welcomed Redman's taunts.

They distracted him from his pain, kept his mind off the drowsiness welling up inside him like warm water filling a tub. He wasn't so far from content.

The dead bodyguard would take explaining. But a paraffin test would reveal that he'd fired a weapon recently, and the gun in Murch's pocket was likely registered to Randolph. Redman's prints on the butt and the fact that Randolph worked for him, together with the bullet in Murch's leg and a clear motive in his testimony in the bribery trial, would put his old boss inside for a long time for attempted murder. "Left here."

The lights of the 14th Precinct were visible down the block. Detective Sergeant Kirdy's precinct, the home of the kind, proud grandfather who had protected Murch during the trial. Murch told Redman to stop the car. It felt good to give him that last order. Charlie Murch had stopped being one of the used.

He recognized Kirdy's blocky shape hastily descending the front steps as he was following Redman out the driver's side and called to him. The sergeant shielded his eyes with one hand against the glare of the headlamps, squinted at the two figures coming toward him, one limping, the other in a bathrobe being pushed out ahead. He drew his magnum from his belt holster. Murch gestured to show friendship. The noise the policeman's gun made was deafening, but Murch never heard it.

"That was quick thinking, sergeant." Hands in the pockets of his robe, Redman looked down at his late captor's body spread-eagled in the gutter. A crowd was gathering.

"We got the squeal on your kidnapping a few minutes ago," Kirdy said. "I was just heading out there when you two showed."

"You ought to make lieutenant for this."

The sergeant's kind eyes glistened. "That'd be great, Mr. Redman. The wife and kids been after me for years to get off the street."

"You will if there's any justice. How's that pretty granddaughter of yours, by the way?"

THE TREE ON EXECUTION HILL

It seemed as if everybody in Good Advice had turned out for the meeting that night in the town hall. Every seat was taken, and the dark oaken rafters hewn and fit in place by the ancestors of a good share of those present resounded with a steady hum of conversation while the broad pine planks that made up the floor creaked beneath the tread of many feet.

Up in front, his plaid jacket thrown back to expose a generous paunch, Carl Lathrop, the town's leading storekeeper and senior member of the council, stood talking with Birdie Flatt from the switchboard. His glasses flashed a Morse code in the bright overhead lights as he settled and resettled them on his fleshy nose. I recognized the gesture from the numerous interviews I had conducted with him as a sign that he was feeling very satisfied with himself, and so I knew what was coming long before most of my neighbors suspected it.

I was something of a freak in the eyes of the citizenry of Good Advice, New Mexico. This was partly because I had been the first person to settle in the area since before 1951, when the aircraft plant had moved on to greener pastures, and partly because, at 42, I was at least ten years younger than anyone else in town. Most people supposed I stayed on out of despair after my wife Sylvia left me to return to civilization, but that wasn't strictly true. We'd originally planned to lay over for a week or two while I collected information for my book and then move on. But then the owner of the town newspaper had died and the paper was put up for sale, and I bought it with the money we'd saved up for the trip. It had been an act of impulse, perhaps a foolish one—certainly it had seemed so to my wife, who had no intention of living so far away from her beloved beauty parlors—but my chief fear in life had always been that I'd miss the big opportunity when it came along. So now I had a news-paper but no Sylvia, which, all things considered, seemed like a pretty fair trade.

The buzz of voices died out as Lathrop took his place behind the lectern. I flipped open my notebook and sat with pencil poised to capture any pearls of wisdom he might have been about to drop.

"We all know why we're here, so we'll dispense with the long-winded introductions." A murmur of approval rippled through the audience. "You've all heard the rumor that the state may build a superhighway near Good Advice," he went on. "Well, it's my pleasant duty to announce that it's no longer a rumor."

Cheers and applause greeted this statement, and it was some minutes before the room grew quiet enough for Lathrop to continue.

"Getting information out of these government fellows is like pulling teeth," he said. "But after about a dozen phone calls to the capital, I finally got hold of the head of the contracting firm that's going to do the job. He told me they plan to start building sometime next fall." He waited until the fresh applause faded, then went on. "Now, this doesn't mean that Good Advice is going to become another Tombstone overnight. When those tourists come streaming in here, we're going to have to be ready for them. That means rezoning for tourist facilities, fixing up our historic landmarks, and so on.

The reason we called this meeting is to decide on ways to make this town appealing to visitors. The floor is open to suggestions."

I spent the next twenty minutes jotting down some of the ideas that came from the enthusiastic citizens. Birdie Flatt was first, with a suggestion that the telephone service be updated, but others disagreed, maintaining that the old upright phones and wall installations found in many of the downtown shops added to the charm of the town. "Uncle Ned" Scoffield, at 97 Good Advice's oldest resident, offered to clean out and fix up the old trading post at the end of Main Street in return for permission to sell his wood carvings and his collection of hand-woven Navajo rugs. Carl Lathrop pledged to turn the old jail, which he had been using as a storeroom, into a tourist attraction. The fact that outlaw Ford Harper had spent his last days there before his hanging, he said, could only add to its popularity. Then, amidst a chorus of groans from scattered parts of the room, Avery Sharecross stood up.

Sharecross was a spindly scarecrow of a man, with an unkempt mane of lusterless black hair spilling over the collar of his frayed sweater and a permanent stoop that made him appear much older than he was. Nobody in town could say how he made his living. Certainly not from the bookstore he had been operating on the corner of Main and Maple for thirty years; there were never any more than two customers in the store at a time, and the prices he charged were so ridiculously low that it was difficult to believe that he managed to break even, let alone show a profit. Everyone was aware of the monthly pension he received from an address in Santa Fe, but no one knew how much it was or why he got it. His bowed shoulders and shuffling gait, the myopia that forced him to squint through the thick lenses of his eyeglasses, the hollows in his pale cheeks were as much a part of the permanent scenery in Good Advice as the burned-out shell of the old flour mill north of town. I closed my notebook and put away my pencil, knowing what he was going to talk about before he opened his mouth. It was all he ever talked about.

Lathrop sighed. "What is it, Avery? As if I didn't know." He rested his chin on one pudgy hand, bracing himself for the ordeal.

"Mr. Chairman, I have a petition." The old bookseller rustled the well-thumbed sheaf of papers he held in one talonlike hand. "I have twenty-six signatures demanding that the citizens of Good Advice vote on whether the tree on Execution Hill be removed."

There was an excited buzz among the spectators. I sat bolt upright in my chair, flipping my notebook back open. How had the old geezer got twenty-five people to agree with him?

For 125 years the tree in question had dominated the high-domed hill two miles outside of town, its skeletal limbs stretching naked against the sky. Of the eighteen trials that had been held in the town hail during the last century, eleven of those tried had ended up swinging from the tree's stoutest limb. It was a favorite spot of mine, an excellent place to sit and meditate. Avery Sharecross, for reasons known only to himself, had been trying to get the council to destroy it for five years. This was the first time he had not stood alone.

Lathrop cleared his throat loudly, probably to cover up his own astonishment. "Now, Avery, you know as well as I do that it takes fifty-five signatures on a petition to raise a vote. You've read the charter."

Sharecross was unperturbed. "When that charter was drafted, Mr. Chairman, this town boasted a population of over fourteen hundred. In the light of our present count, I believe that provision can be waived." He struck the pages with his finger-tips. "These signatures represent nearly one-tenth of the local voting public. They have a right to be heard."

"How come you're so fired up to see that tree reduced to kindling, anyway? What's the difference to your?"

"That tree"—Sharecross flung a scrawny arm in the direction of the nearest window—"represents a time in this town's history when lynch law reigned and pompous hypocrites sentenced their peers to death regardless of their innocence or guilt." His cheeks were flushed now, his eyes ablaze behind the bottle-glass spectacles. "That snarl of dead limbs has been a blemish on the smooth face of this community for over a hundred years, and it's about time we got rid of it."

It was an impressive performance, and he sounded sincere, but I wasn't buying it. Good Advice, after all, had not been my first exposure to journalism. After you've been in this business awhile, you get a feeling for when someone is telling the truth, and Sharecross wasn't. Whatever reasons he had for wishing to destroy the town's oldest landmark, they had nothing to do with any sense of injustice. Of that I was certain.

Lathrop sighed. "All right, Avery, let's see your petition. If the signatures check out, we'll vote." Once the papers were in his hands, Lathrop called the other members of the town council around him to look them over. Finally he motioned them back to their seats and turned back toward the lectern. For the next half hour he read off the names on the petition—many of which surprised me, for they included some of the town's leading citizens—to make sure the signatures were genuine. Every one of those mentioned spoke up to assure him that they were. At length the storekeeper laid the pages down.

"Before we vote," he said, "the floor is open to dissenting opinions.—Mr. Macklin?"

My hand had gone up before he finished speaking. I got to my feet, conscious of all the eyes upon me.

"No one is arguing what Mr. Sharecross said about the injustices done in the past," I began haltingly. "But tearing down something that's a large part of our history won't change anything." I paused, searching for words. I was a lot more eloquent behind a typewriter. "Mr. Sharecross says the tree reminds us of the sordid past. I think that's as it should be. A nagging reminder of a time when we weren't so noble is a healthy thing to have in our midst. I wouldn't want to live in a society that kicked its mistakes under the rug."

The words were coming easier now. "There's been a lot of talk here tonight about promoting tourist trade. Well, destroying a spot where eleven infamous badmen met their reward is one sure way of aborting any claims we might have had upon shutter-happy visitors." I shook my head emphatically, a gesture left over from my college debating-club days. "History is too precious for us to turn our backs on it, for whatever reason. Sharecross and his sympathizers would do well to realize that our true course calls for us to turn our gaze forward and forget about rewriting the past."

There was some applause as I sat down, but it died out when Sharecross seized the floor again. "I'm not a Philistine, Mr. Chairman," he said calmly. "Subject to the will of the council, I hereby pledge the sum of five thousand dollars for the erection of a statue of Enoch Howard, Good Advice's founder, atop Execution Hill once the tree has been removed. I, too, have some feeling for history." His eyes slid in my direction.

That was dirty pool, I thought as he took his seat amid thunderous cheering from those present. In one way or another, Enoch Howard's blood flowed in the veins of over a third of the population of Good Advice. Now I knew how he had obtained those signatures. But why? What did he hope to gain?

"What about expense?" someone said.

"No problem," countered Sharecross, on his feet again. "Floyd Kramer there has offered to bulldoze down the tree and cart it away at cost."

"That true, Floyd?" Lathrop asked.

A heavy-jowled man in a blue work shirt buttoned to the neck gave him the high sign from his standing position near the door.

I shot out of my chair again, but this time my eyes were directed upon my skeletal opponent and not the crowd. "I've fought you in print and on the floor of the town hail over this issue," I told him, "and if necessary I'll keep on fighting you right to the top of Execution Hill. I don't care how many statues you pull out of your hat; you won't get away with whatever it is you're trying to do."

The old bookseller made no reply. His eyes were blank behind his spectacles. I sat back down.

I could see that Lathrop's attitude had changed, for he had again taken to raising and lowering his eyeglasses confidently upon the bridge of his nose. Enoch Howard was his great-grandfather on his mother's side. "Now we'll vote," he said. "All those in favor of removing the tree on Execution Hill to make room for a statue of Enoch Howard signify by saying aye."

Rain was hissing on the grass when I parked my battered pickup truck at the bottom of the hill and got out to fetch the shovel out of the back. It was a long climb to the top and I was out of shape, but I didn't want to risk leaving telltale ruts behind by driving up the slope. Halfway up my feet began to feel like lead and the blood was pounding in my ears like a pneumatic hammer; by the time I found myself at the base of the deformed tree I had barely enough energy left to find the spot I wanted and begin digging. It was dark, and the soil was soaked just enough so that each time I took out a shovelful the hole filled up again, with the result that it was ten minutes before I made any progress at all. After half an hour I stopped to rest. That's when all the lights came on and turned night into day.

The headlights of half a dozen automobiles were trained full upon me. For a fraction of a second I stood unmoving, frozen with shock. Then I hurled the shovel like a javelin at the nearest light and started to run. The first step I took landed in the hole. I fell headlong to the ground, emptying my lungs and twisting my ankle painfully. When I looked up, I was surrounded by people.

"I've waited five years for this." The voice belonged to Avery Sharecross.

"How did you know?" I said when I found my breath.

"I never did. Not for sure." Sharecross was standing over me now, an avenging angel wearing a threadbare coat and scarf. "I once heard that you spent all the money you had on the newspaper. If that was true, I wondered what your wife used for bus fare back to Santa Fe when she left you. Everyone knew you argued with her bitterly over your decision to stay. That you lost control and murdered her seemed obvious to me.

"I decided you buried her at the foot of the hanging tree, which was the reason you spent more time here than anyone else. The odds weren't in favor of my obtaining permission to dig up the hill because of mere supposition, so it became necessary to catch you in the act of unearthing her yourself. That's when I got the idea to propose removing the tree and force you to find someplace else to dispose of the body."

He turned to a tall man whose Stetson glistened wetly in the unnatural illumination of the headlights at his back. "Sheriff, if your men will resume digging where Mr. Macklin left off, it's my guess you'll find the corpse of Sylvia Macklin before morning. I retired from the Santa Fe Police Department long before they felt the need to teach us anything about reading rights to those we arrested, so perhaps you'll oblige."

LOCK, STOCK, AND CASKET

People who didn't know that Umberto Fugurello was a great artist tended to mistake him for a comical old man. Outside his shop, his was a rheumatic figure smaller than the average in a tight black coat buttoned only at the neck and a gray homburg perched atop wild gray hair like an egg in a nest. Below that were gold-rimmed spectacles, a tight, lipless mouth, and a chin that usually wore a Band-aid to remind him that one can get only so many shaves out of a razor before it becomes a lethal weapon.

In the shop, he was a professional in leather apron and shirt-sleeves, the latter rolled up past corded forearms ending in large hands cracked and discolored by the many stains and acids with which he worked. The walls and benches twinkled with mallets, chisels, miters, and wood augers of spotless nickel steel, no two of which were designed for the same purpose. Their handles were worn to fit the contours of Umberto's calloused fingers and no one else's.

Umberto Fugurello made caskets. So had every previous male Fugurello back to Great-Great-Grandfather Filberto Gugliamo, who crafted the final resting place of Catherine de Medici. Since then, many another famous figure had gone to his reward in vessels fashioned by the Stradivari of caskets, and Umberto, had he been a boastful man, could point with pride to mausoleums and family vaults throughout both hemispheres in which resided the evidence, but it was generally agreed within the closed ranks of the world's casket makers that Umberto was the best of his line. Who could forget the Egyptian-style sarcophagus he had designed for the eminent archaeologist Professor Simon Broderick, dead of a hitherto unknown Middle Eastern strain of venereal disease, or the gold inlays around the lid of the box in which Dirk Crandall, the motion picture star, was buried after his wife caught him rehearsing a love scene from his new movie with a studio switchboard operator, or the lion motif Umberto had created for famed animal tamer Hugo von Rasmussen following that tragic episode involving a young Siberian tiger the performer had mistaken for an aging Bengal? There was also the double-decked piece he had built on commission for a local Syndicate chief, but that was known only to Umberto himself, and he was not one to boast.

In any case, past triumphs meant nothing to him. He lived in the present. And why not, in view of the fact that he was working on his masterpiece?

It lay across two sawhorses in the back room of the shop, a lozenge-shaped construction without a nail or a corner or a sharp edge anywhere. The handles were solid gold, the lining deep blue satin. The crowning touch—the Fugurello family crest, a hammer in a mailed fist framed in casket shape—was assuming definition even now at the point of Umberto's chisel. It surpassed all his earlier achievements, and certainly nothing would ever rival it in the future. For this was to be his own casket.

The imminence of death hardly saddened him. He was 78 after all, and more aware than most that no one lived forever.

His only regret was that he would be unable to observe the reaction to his last and greatest work when it was unveiled at his funeral. He was lamenting this necessary disappointment when the little bell mounted on the front door of the shop announced a visitor.

"Uncle Umberto?" called a familiar voice.

The old man drew a tarpaulin over the casket just as his nephew, the mortician, entered through the curtain that separated the two rooms. The visitor was tall and thin—one was tempted to say "cadaverous"—and wore his dark hair fashionably long. Recent cosmetic surgery on his nose had left him with average features dominated by icy blue eyes that matched his suit.

"Good morning, Antonio."

"Tony." Something like annoyance edged the young man's cool tone. "Tony Farrell. I had it changed, remember?"

"Who could forget?" The decision to forsake the honored family name had possibly contributed to the early demise of Antonio's father, brother of Umberto. "What brings you to my shop on a Saturday morning?"

"You mean my shop."

His uncle said nothing. That had been a great mistake, his deeding the property over to his brother's son on the occasion of his birth. Umberto had not touched wine since that night.

Antonio said, "A fellow has a right to inspect his possessions from time to time. What's this, another masterpiece?" Before Umberto could stop him he reached out and pulled-off the tarpaulin.

For a moment the beauty of the thing struck even Antonio. But he recovered himself quickly. "That's real gold in the trimming!" he complained. "What good will that do anyone when it's in the ground? What did I tell you about throwing money away on materials we don't need?"

"My money, not yours. The materials came out of my savings."

"And whose time did you spend on it? I heard you were turning down business, but I didn't believe it until now. That's the family crest on the lid. What were you going to do, enter it in some fool exhibition put on by those graveworms you call your colleagues?"

Umberto made no reply. In a twinkling, his nephew's manner went from hot to cold. "We'll talk about this later. I came down here to tell you I'm selling the shop."

"Selling!" The old man pronounced it as if it were an unfamiliar word.

"Lock, stock, and casket. I'm liquidating the inventory and putting the building and property on the open market. That includes your little project here. It should bring several thousand once we scrape off the engraving."

"We have been in this business for—"

"Too long," Antonio interrupted. "It's called moving with the times. No one does business with independents anymore. They go to the big supply houses, where they can get machine-made models for a fraction of what you charge. This is a prime location for a parking lot. Of course, that means tearing down the building, but that shouldn't cost too much. A swift kick will do it. I'll make a killing."

"And me, Antonio?"

"Tony," snapped the other.

"Will you tear me down too, or sell me along with the inventory?"

His nephew smiled—a mortician's smile, blandly obsequious. "Certainly not, Uncle. You've worked hard all your life; you've earned a rest. I've made arrangements with the Waning Years Retirement Home. You move in next week."

"But I don't want to retire!"

"What you want or don't want is not an issue. As your only living relative, I can have you declared incapable of caring for yourself and commit you to a state institution. Instead I've elected to place you in private hands. You should be grateful."

"I'll fight you! I'll hire a lawyer."

"And what will you use to pay him? You don't even own these tools—which, by the way, I have a buyer for, if you can provide a list of what you have here. If you can't, I'll just make one." He produced a pad and pencil.

"I have rights."

"Not if you're senile, and that's what I'll prove in court if you insist upon making things difficult. This is a young man's world, Uncle Umberto. If you hadn't been so busy making your pretty boxes you'd know that. Now, try to stay out of my way while I inventory this equipment." He started counting the braces and bits on the wall behind the lathe, tallying them into his pad.

Umberto glared at his nephew's back. Then his eyes fell to his masterpiece's unfinished crest, and as always when he contemplated a project, all other cares receded. He picked up the No. 5 hammer he had been using, thought better of it, exchanged it for a heavier No. 3 with a shiny Neoprine grip, and brought it down with all his might squarely into the center of Antonio's fashionable hairstyle.

The Fugurello sanity hearing is in the records for anyone who cares to review it. Following conflicting testimonies by the psychiatrists who had examined the defendant, a harried judge ruled him legally insane and unfit for trial and committed him to the state mental institution for treatment. This failed to cheer Umberto, who was depressed by his inability to attend his nephew's celebrated funeral.

The centerpiece was the talk of his profession for weeks.

Under a rose-colored spot, the casket's eggshell finish threw off a high gleam that put the flowers to shame. Everyone agreed that Antonio had never looked better, and when the service was over and the top half of the lid was lowered, exposing the ornate crest, the guests were moved in spite of the solemnity of the occasion to applaud.

After eighteen months, authorities at the institution agreed that Umberto could be trusted with tools once again, and he was granted permission to do light work in the shop. These were happy days for Umberto, who had been cheered by his colleagues' letters and telegrams of congratulation upon his masterpiece; doing work he loved, he no longer thought about death or its proximity. The doctors had in fact given him a clean bill of health, which he attributed to freedom from the responsibility of earning a living.

Then came the untimely passing of the institution's director and a special request for Umberto to craft a vessel for the remains. Material posed a problem in the face of bureaucratic cutbacks, but with effort he managed to obtain some good cedar and recycled brass for the handles and fittings. Making something worthwhile out of such second-class stock was a challenge he welcomed.

He rubbed the last irregularity from the surface and stood back to survey his workmanship. The trimming glittered like gold against the deep red-brown of the wood. He frowned appreciably at his reflection in the finish. It wasn't a masterpiece, but it was still good craftsmanship, and that was something money couldn't buy.

BAD BLOOD

Light spread gray through the sycamores, igniting billions of hanging droplets with the black trunks standing among them looking not fixed to the earth but suspended from above like stalactites. A mockingbird awoke to release its complex scan into the sopping air. There was no answer and the song was not repeated. Leaves crackled, drying.

The man was already awake, a tense silhouette against a yellowing sun louvered by vertical tree shafts, a knee on the ground, the other drawn up to his chest and one fist wrapped around a rifle with its butt planted in the moist earth. His profile was sharp, with a pointed nose like a check mark, the angle dramatized by a long stiff bill tilting down from a green cap with JOHN DEERE embossed in block letters on a patch on the front of the crown. His shirt was coarse and blue under a red and black checked jacket with darns on the elbows. His jeans had been blue but were now earth-colored, like his boots under their cake of silver clay. He had been there in that position since an hour before dawn.

From where he was crouched, the ground fell off forty-five degrees to a berry thicket that girdled the mountain. The thicket had been transplanted by his great-grandfather from a nearby bog and allowed to grow wild until it resembled the tangled barbed wire in which the great-grandfather's son would snare himself thirty years later and wait for the sun to rise and the Germans to discover him in a muddy place called Ypres. This natural barrier had trapped a number of local men the same way, to wait like the soldier and, now, like the soldier's grandson for the dawn and what the dawn would bring. The slope bristled with leafed trees and cedars and twisted jackpines, heirs to the great towering monarchs that had fallen to the timber boom of another century, whose black stumps still dotted the mountain-side like rotted teeth.

A third of the way down the slope, a hundred feet below him and two hundred feet above the thicket, stood his own shack. It had been built of logs when James Monroe was president, but a later ancestor had nailed clapboard over the logs to make it resemble a proper house. A four-paned window that had been covered with oiled paper before the coming of the railroad now reflected sunlight from three panes, emphasizing the blank space where a bullet had shattered the glass.

Now, as the sun lifted, its light struck sparks off tiny fragments on his jeans. He flicked them away carefully. Before tumbling out of the shack he had made sure to remove his wristwatch and anything else that might catch light and betray him.

He knew who had fired the bullet. Inside the shack, its cracked black cover freshly nicked by that same projectile, lay a Bible as thick as a man's thigh, its cream flyleaves scribbled over in old brown ink with names of his forebears and the dates of their lives and deaths going back to 1789, when an inden-tured servant from Cornwall bought the book second-hand in London and recorded the birth of a son named Jotham. Four generations of names followed before the simple entry: "Eben Candler, murdered by Ezekiel Finlayson, Hawkins County,

Kentucky, May 11, 1882. His will be done." Eighteen similar notations appeared on succeeding pages, in differing hands, until the survivors wearied of keeping count. The final line, "Jotham Edward Candler, born September 8, 1951," written in his father's formal script, commemorated his own birth. Finlayson losses were not included.

No one remembered the specifics of that first encounter between a Candler and a Finlayson, although it had something to do with the ownership of forty acres of bottom land in Unico County. Only the casualties were remembered. Jotham's own coming of age had been marked by a daily catechism in which he was expected to recite, in what ever order asked, the names of the Candler slain, their murderers, and the dates of their deaths as they had been recorded in the big Bible; and when he was strong enough to lift a squirrel rifle, he had been taught to think of his small, furry targets not as squirrels, but as Finlaysons.

It did not matter that no one knew who held title to those forty acres—that was as gone as the bottomland itself, seized by the bank during the depression of 1893—or that the fecundity of the Candler and Finlayson women had led to considerable interbreeding between the two families during the long truces. Hatred was an inheritance as solid and treasured as the old Bible and Great Grandmother Candler's homely samplers, their red embroidery and white linen gone the same dead-skin brown on the walls of the tiny shack. Jotham, with a bachelor's degree in agriculture and three years in Vietnam behind him, was growing marijuana on plots that had supported his father's stills, and the Finlaysons had sold Ezekiel's ferrier's shop to buy a funeral home and the first of a chain of hardware stores, but aside from that little had changed. Bad blood was bad always.

As the sun cleared the mountain, its light turned leafy green coming down through the branches. Creatures stirred in the dry-shuck mattress of last year's leaves, and the last wisp of woodsmoke left the shack's chimney in a bit of shredded tissue that vanished into the thatch of fog now treetop-high as it lifted and broke apart. Jotham's assailant would know by that that he was no longer inside. The waiting was almost ended.

Jotham was the last Candler to bear that surname. His sisters were married and his only brother had died in Korea before Jotham was old enough to remember him. He would carry the name to the grave with him because of what the army's defoliants had done to his genes in Da Nang. In view of that temptation—the opportunity to wipe out by one death the long line of Candlers—young Bertram Finlayson's attempt to kill him in his sleep that morning seemed long overdue.

For he had no doubt it was Bertram.

Eight years Jotham's junior, he had been too young to serve in Vietnam, and had spent that frustration in turkey shoots across the state, winning a caseful of trophies to display under the antlered heads on the walls of his fine house in town. His arsenal was a legend among collectors of firearms and he often boasted that he had used them to kill every kind of animal that lived in the county but one. He was the only Finlayson young enough and mean enough to bother about a fight that most had thought was buried with Jotham's father.

Several times since Jotham had returned from college, Bertram had tried to draw him into something in town, from which Jotham had always walked away. Witnesses said it was because he had had enough of killing in Asia. But those who said that were thinking of other wars, did not understand that the object of his had been to stay alive; killing came secondary, if at all. And now here he was, twelve years and ten thousand miles later, trying to stay alive in another jungle.

A squirrel began chattering, a high-pitched coughing noise

like a small engine trying to start. Something was annoying it. Not him; the squirrel was too far away, high in an ash on the other side of the shack. He spotted its humped profile on the side of the trunk sixty feet up and scanned the ground at the base. A treefall twenty yards down the slope looked promising. He raised the 30.06 and lined up the iron sights and sent a bullet into the center of the fall. Something jumped, startled. Dead leaves rattled on the inert branches.

The echo of his first report was still snarling in the distance when he fired again, into those moving leaves. Almost instantly, a section of bark on a cedar a foot to Jotham's right exploded in a cloud of splinters, followed quickly by the crack of a .30-30. He hurled himself and his weapon headlong down the slope, rolling and coming up on the other side of a clump of suckers grown up around a pine stump. The squirrel had stopped chattering.

Bertram was a cooler hand than he'd thought. After the first shot he had waited, then fired at Jotham's second muzzle flash.

Again the waiting began.

Once, after exchanging fire with a Cong he had never seen, Jotham had waited for eleven hours in a fog of mosquitoes and heavy air, unmoving, his survival dependent upon his either killing the guerrilla or boring him into moving on. At the end the Cong had lost patience first, and when he rose from cover to investigate, Jotham had taken his head off with a burst from his M-16. How to wait was the hardest lesson of all. He settled himself on his other knee to give that haunch a rest.

The sun climbed into a thin sheeting of clouds that parted from time to time, changing the light as in an ancient motion picture. The air warmed, grew hot and thick. Twice he was attacked by wood ticks, once on the back of a hand, the other time, very painfully, on his neck. He did not move to brush them away.

When the sun was directly overhead, he knew a terrible urge to get up and find out if Bertram was still there. More than the heat it made the sweat stand out in burrs on his forehead and greased his armpits and crotch. It must have been what the Cong felt just before he committed suicide.

But Jotham held his position and it subsided.

No one came up the mountain. In other years, uninvited visitors had met moon-shiners' buckshot, and now even the authorities counseled against wandering the hills and chancing the protective wrath of marijuana growers and mad survivalists.

Around midafternoon the sky darkened and big drops pattered the leaves on the ground and rolled along the edge of the bill of Jotham's cap and hung quivering before falling to his raised thigh with loud plops. He swung the rifle horizontal to keep moisture out of the barrel. But the rain passed swiftly. A rainbow arched over the shack and melted away.

The air cooled toward dusk. Bertram would have to move soon. Jotham's new knowledge of his enemy's instincts told him that he would not again risk darkness in the woods with an experienced jungle fighter. Jotham reversed legs again, working the stiffness out of the long muscles in his thighs.

The woods to the west were catching fire in the lowering sun when a buck muledeer that Jotham had never heard went crashing off through the woods on the opposite side of the shack, blatting a warning to others of its kind. At that moment the treefall shook and a pair of bull shoulders with a hatless head nestled in between reared against a sky striped with tree trunks. Light sheared along something long and shiny.

Jotham raised his rifle without aiming, trusting to the barrel to find its mark because he could no longer see the front sight, and touched the trigger. The butt pulsed against his shoulder, but he did not hear the blast. It had been that way when he'd killed the Cong. In roaring silence the bull shoulders hunched and the hatless head went back and the silhouette crumpled in on itself like a balloon deflating. The long and shiny thing flashed, falling.

Jotham let the sun slip to a red crescent before rising. In gray light he approached the treefall, lifting his feet clear of the old stumps more from memory than from sight, his eyes fixed on the dark thing draped over the treefall with the .30-30 on the ground in front of it. Carefully he used a foot to slide the rifle further out of the reach of the dangling hands, then took another step and grasped a handful of straw-colored hair and raised a slack face with open eyes and mouth into the last ray of light. It was Bertram Finlayson.

He let the face drop and started down the mountain toward town to tell his sister Lucy that she was a widow.

STATE OF GRACE

"Ralph? This is Lyla."

"Who the hell is Lyla?"

"Lyla Dane. I live in the apartment above you, for chrissake. We see each other every day."

"The hooker."

"You live over a dirty bookstore. What do you want for a neighbor, a freaking rocket scientist?"

Ralph Poteet sat up in bed and rumpled his mouse-colored hair. He fumbled the alarm clock off the night table and held it very close to his good eye. He laid it facedown and scowled at the receiver in his hand. "It's two-thirty ayem."

"Thanks. My watch stopped and I knew if I called you you'd tell me what time it is. Listen, you're like a cop, right?"

"Not at two-thirty ayem."

"I'll give you a hundred dollars to come up here now." He blew his nose on the sheet. "Ain't that supposed to be the other way around?"

"You coming up or not? You're not the only dick in town. I just called you because you're handy."

"What's the squeal?"

"I got a dead priest in my bed."

He said he was on his way and hung up. A square gin bottle slid off the blanket. He caught it before it hit the floor, but it was empty and he dropped it. He put on his Tyrolean hat with a feather in the band, found his suitpants on the floor half under the bed, and pulled them on over his pajamas. He stuck bare feet into his loafers and because it was October he pulled on his suitcoat, grunting with the effort. He was forty-three years old and forty pounds overweight. He looked for his gun just because it was 2:30 a.m., couldn't find it, and went out.

Lyla Dane was just five feet and ninety pounds in a pink kimono and slippers with carnations on the toes. She wore her black hair in a pageboy like Anna May Wong, but the Oriental effect fell short of her round Occidental face. "You look like crap," she told Ralph at the door.

"That's what two hours' sleep will do for you. Where's the hundred?"

"Don't you want to see the stiff first?"

"What do I look like, a pervert?"

"Yes." She opened a drawer in the telephone stand and counted a hundred in twenties and tens into his palm.

He stuck the money in a pocket and followed her through a small living room decorated by K-Mart into a smaller bedroom containing a Queen Anne bed that had cost twice as much as all the other furniture combined and took up most of the space in the room. The rest of the space was taken up by Monsignor John Breame, pastor of St. Boniface, a cathedral Ralph sometimes used to exchange pictures for money, although not so much lately because the divorce business was on the slide. He recognized the monsignor's pontifical belly under the flesh-colored satin sheet that barely covered it. The monsignor's face was purple.

"He a regular?" Ralph found a Diamond matchstick in his suitcoat pocket and stuck the end between his teeth.

"Couple of times a month. Tonight I thought he was breathing a little hard after. Then he wasn't."

"What do you want me to do?"

"Get rid of him, what else? Cops find him here the Christers'll run me out on a cross. I got a business to run."

"Cost you another hundred."

"I just gave you a hundred."

"You're lucky I don't charge by the pound. Look at that gut."

"You look at it. He liked the missionary position."

"What else would he?"

She got the hundred and gave it to him. He told her to leave. "Where'll I go?"

"There's beds all over town. You probably been in half of them. Or go find an all-night movie if you don't feel like working. Don't come back before dawn."

She dressed and went out after emptying the money drawer into a shoulder bag she took with her. When she was gone Ralph helped himself to a Budweiser from her refrigerator and looked up a number in the city directory and called it from the telephone in the living room. A voice like ground glass answered.

"Bishop Stoneman?" Ralph asked.

"It's three ayem," said the voice.

"Thank you. My name is Ralph Poteet. I'm a private detective. I'm sorry to have to inform you Monsignor Breame is dead."

"Mary Mother of God! What happened?"

"I'm no expert. It looks like a heart attack."

"Mary Mother of God. In bed?"

"Yeah."

"Was he—do you know if he was in a state of grace?"

"That's what I wanted to talk to you about," Ralph said.

*   *   *

The man Bishop Stoneman sent was tall and gaunt, with a complexion like wet pulp and colorless hair cropped down to stubble. He had on a black coat buttoned to the neck and looked like an early martyr. He said his name was Morgan. Together they wrapped the monsignor in the soiled bedding and carried him down three flights of stairs, stopping a dozen times to rest, and laid him on the back seat of a big Buick Electra parked between streetlamps. Ralph stood guard at the car while Morgan went back up for the monsignor's clothes. It was nearly 4:00 a.m. and their only witness was a skinny cat who lost interest after a few minutes and stuck one leg up in the air to lick itself.

After a long time Morgan came down and threw the bundle onto the front seat and gave Ralph an envelope containing a hundred dollars. He said he'd handle it from there. Ralph watched him drive off and went back up to bed, He was very tired and didn't wake up until the fire sirens were grinding down in front of the building. He hadn't even heard the explosion when Lyla Dane returned to her apartment at dawn.

"Go away."

"That's no way to talk to your partner," Ralph said.

"Ex-partner. You got the boot and I did, too. Now I'm giving it to you. Go away."

Dale English was a special investigator with the sheriff's department who kept his office in the City-County Building. He had a monolithic face and fierce black eyebrows like Lincoln's, creating an effect he tried to soften with pink shirts and knobby knitted ties. He and Ralph had shared a city prowl car for two years, until some evidence turned up missing from the property room. Both had been dismissed, English without prejudice because unlike the case with Ralph, none of the incriminating items had been found in English's possession.

"The boot didn't hurt you none," Ralph said.

"No, it just cost me my wife and my kid and seven years' seniority. I'd be a lieutenant now."

Ralph lowered his bulk onto the vinyl-and-aluminum chair in front of English's desk. "I wouldn't hang this on you if I could go to the city cops. Somebody's out to kill me."

"Tell whoever it is I said good luck."

"I ain't kidding."

"Me neither."

"You know that hooker got blown up this morning?"

"The gas explosion? I read about it."

"Yeah, well, it wasn't no accident. I'm betting the arson boys find a circuit breaker in the wall switch. You know what that means."

"Sure. Somebody lets himself in and turns on the gas and puts a breaker in the switch so when the guy comes home the spark blows him to hell. What was the hooker into and what was your angle?"

"It's more like who was into the hooker." Ralph told him the rest.

"This the same Monsignor Breame was found by an altar boy counting angels in his bed at the St. Bonjface rectory this morning?" English asked.

"Thanks to me and this bug Morgan."

"So what do you want?"

"Hell, protection. The blowup was meant for me. Morgan thought I'd be going back to that same apartment and set it up while I was waiting for him to come down with Breame's clothes."

"Bishops don't kill people over priests that can't keep their vows in their pants."

Ralph screwed up his good eye. Its mate looked like a sour ball someone had spat out. "What world you living in? Shape the Church is in, he'd do just that to keep it quiet."

"Go away, Ralph."

"Well, pick up Morgan at least. He can't be hard to find. He looks like one of those devout creeps you see skulking around in paintings of the Crucifixion."

"I don't have any jurisdiction in the city."

"That ain't why you won't do it. Hey, I told IAD you didn't have nothing to do with what went down in Property."

"It would've carried more weight if you'd submitted to a lie detector test. Mine was inconclusive." He paged through a report on his desk without looking at it. "I'll run the name Morgan and the description you gave me through the computer and see what it coughs up. There won't be anything."

"Thanks, buddy."

"You sure you didn't take pictures? It'd be your style to try and put the squeeze on a bishop."

"I thought about it, but my camera's in hock." Ralph got up. "You can get me at my place. They got the fire out before it reached my floor."

"That was lucky. Gin flames are the hardest to put out."

He was driving a brand-new red Riviera he had promised to sell for a lawyer friend who was serving two years for suborning to commit perjury, only he hadn't gotten around to it yet. He parked in a handicapped zone near his building and climbed stairs smelling of smoke and firemen's rubber boots. Inside his apartment, which was also his office, he rewound the tape on his answering machine and played back a threatening call from a loan shark named Zwingman, a reminder from a dentist's receptionist with a NutraSweet voice that last month's root canal was still unpaid for, and a message from a heavy breather that he had to play back three times before deciding it was a man. He was staring toward the door, his attention on the tape, when a square of white paper slithered over the threshold.

That day he was wearing his legal gun, a short-nosed .38 Colt, in a clip on his belt, and an orphan High Standard .22 magnum derringer in an ankle holster. Drawing the Colt, he lunged and tore open the door just in time to hear the Street door closing below. He swung around and crossed to the street window. Through it he saw a narrow figure in a long black coat and the back of a close-cropped head crossing against traffic to the other side. The man rounded the corner and vanished.

Ralph holstered the revolver and picked up the note. it was addressed to him in a round, shaped hand.

Mr. Poteet:

    If it is not inconvenient, your presence at my home could prove to your advantage and mine. Cordially,

                    Philip Stoneman, Bishop-in-Ordinary

Clipped to it was a hundred-dollar bill.

Bishop Stoneman lived in a refurbished brownstone in a neighborhood that the city had reclaimed from slum by evicting its residents and sandblasting graffiti off the buildings. The bell was answered by a youngish bald man in a dark suit and clerical collar who introduced himself as Brother Edwards and directed Ralph to a curving staircase, then retired to be seen no more. Ralph didn't hear Morgan climbing behind him until something hard probed his right kidney. A hand patted him down and removed the Colt from its clip. "End of the hail."

The bishop was a tall old man, nearly as thin as Morgan, with iron-gray hair and a face that fell away to the white shackle of his collar. He rose from behind a redwood desk to greet his visitor in an old-fashioned black frock that made him look like a crow. The room was large and square and smelled of leather from the books on the built-in shelves and pipe tobacco. Morgan entered behind Ralph and closed the door.

"Thank you for coming, Mr. Poteet. Please sit down."

"Thank Ben Franklin." But he settled into a deep leather chair that gripped his buttocks like a big hand in a soft glove.

"I'm grateful for this chance to thank you in person," Stoneman said, sitting in his big swivel. "I'm very disappointed in Monsignor Breame. I'd hoped that he would take my place at the head of the diocese."

"You bucking for cardinal?"

He smiled. "I suppose you've shown yourself worthy of confidence. Yes, His Holiness has offered me the red hat. The appointment will be announced next month."

"That why you tried to croak me? I guess your right bower cashing in in a hooker's bed would look bad in Rome."

One corner of the desk supported a silver tray containing two long-stemmed glasses and a cut-crystal decanter half full of ruby liquid. Stoneman removed the stopper and filled both glasses. "This is an excellent Madeira. I confess that the austere life allows me two mild vices. The other is tobacco."

"What are we celebrating?" Ralph didn't pick up his glass.

"Your new appointment as chief of diocesan security. The position pays well and the hours are regular."

"In return for which I forget about Monsignor Breame?"

"And entrust all related material to me. You took pictures, of course." Stoneman sipped from his glass.

Ralph lifted his. "I'd be pretty stupid not to, considering what happened to Lyla Dane."

"I heard about the tragedy. That child's soul could have been saved."

"You should've thought about that before your boy Morgan croaked her." Ralph gulped off half his wine. It tasted bitter.

The bishop laid a bony hand atop an ancient ornate Bible on the desk. His guest thought he was about to swear his innocence. "This belonged to St. Thomas. More, not Aquinas. I have a weakness for religious antiques."

"Thought you only had two vices." The air in the room stirred slightly. Ralph turned to see who had entered, but his vision was thickening. Morgan was a shimmering shadow. The glass dropped from Ralph's hand. He bent to retrieve it and came up with the derringer. Stoneman's shout echoed. Ralph fired twice at the shadow and pitched headfirst into its depths.

He awoke feeling pretty much the way he did most mornings, with his head throbbing and his stomach turning over. He wanted to turn over, with it, but he was stretched out on a hard, flat surface with his ankles strapped down and his arms tied above his head. He was looking up at water-stained tile. His joints ached.

"The sedative was in the stem of your glass," Stoneman was saying. He was out of Ralph's sight and Ralph had the impression he'd been talking for a while. "You've been out for two hours. The unpleasant effect is temporary, rather like a hangover."

"Did I get him?" Ralph's tongue moved sluggishly. "No, you missed rather badly. It required persuasion to get Morgan to carry you down here to the basement instead of killing you on the spot. He was quite upset." Ralph squirmed. There was something familiar about the position he was tied in. For some reason he thought of Mrs. Thornton, his ninth-grade American Lit. teacher. What is the significance of Poe's "Pit and the Pendulum" to the transcendentalist movement? His organs shriveled.

"Another antique," said the bishop. "The Inquisition did not end when General Lasalle entered Madrid, but went on for several years in the provinces. This particular rack was still in use after Torquemada's death. The gears are original. The wheel is new, and of course I had to replace the ropes. Morgan?"

A shoe scraped the floor and a spoked shadow fluttered across Ralph's vision. His arms tightened. He gasped.

"That's enough. We don't want to put Mr. Poteet back under." To Ralph: "Morgan just returned from your apartment. He found neither pictures nor film nor even a camera. Where are they?"

"I was lying. I didn't take no pictures."

"Morgan."

Ralph shrieked.

"Enough! His Holiness is sensitive about scandal, Mr. Poteet. I won't have Monsignor Breame's indiscretions bar me from the Vatican. Who is keeping the pictures for you?"

"There ain't no pictures, honest."

"Morgan!"

A socket started to slip. Ralph screamed and blubbered.

"Enough!" Stoneman's fallen-away face moved into Ralph's vision. His eyes were fanatic. "A few more turns will sever your spine. You could be spoon-fed for the rest of your life. Do you think that after failing to kill you in that apartment I would hesitate to cripple you? Where are the pictures?"

"I didn't take none!"

"Morgan!"

"No!" It ended in a howl. His armpits were on fire. The ropes creaked.

"Police! Don't move!"

The bishop's face jerked away. The spoked shadow fluttered. The tension went out of Ralph's arms suddenly, and relief poured into his joints. A shot flattened the air. Two more answered it. Something struck the bench Ralph was lying on and drove a splinter into his back. He thought at first he was shot, but the pain was nothing.; he'd just been through worse. He squirmed onto his hip and saw Morgan, one black-clad arm stained and glistening, leveling a heavy automatic at a target behind Ralph's back. Scrambling out of the line of fire, Ralph jerked his bound hands and the rack's wheel, six feet in diameter with handles bristling from it like a ship's helm, spun around. One of the handles slapped the gun from Morgan's hand. Something cracked past Ralph's left ear and Morgan fell back against the tile wall and slid down it. The shooting stopped.

Ralph wriggled onto his other hip. A man he didn't know in a houndstooth coat with a revolver in his hand had Bishop Stoneman spread-eagled against a wall and was groping in his robes for weapons. Dale English came off the stairs with the Ruger he had been carrying since Ralph was his partner. He bent over Morgan on the floor, then straightened and holstered the gun. He looked at Ralph. "I guess you're okay."

"I am if you got a pocketknife."

"Arson boys found the circuit breaker in the wall switch just like you said." He cut Ralph's arms free and sawed through the straps on his ankles. "When you didn't answer your telephone I went to your place and found Stoneman's note."

"He confessed to the hooker's murder."

"I know. I heard him."

"How the hell long were you listening?"

"We had to have enough to pin him to it, didn't we?"

"You son of a bitch. You just wanted to hear me holler."

"Couldn't help it. You sure got lungs."

"I got to go to the toilet."

"Stick around after," English said. "I need a statement to hand to the city boys. They won't like County sticking its face in this."

Ralph hobbled upstairs. When he was through in the bathroom he found his hat and coat and headed out. At the front door he turned around and went back into the bishop's study, where he hoisted Thomas More's Bible under one arm. He knew a bookseller who would probably give him at least a hundred for it.

DIMINISHED CAPACITY

I was halfway through my third ham sandwich when the intercom on my desk razzed. Angrily, I choked down the mouthful I was working on and punched the speaker button, which was too small for my rather broad thumb.

"Sharon, I thought I told you never to interrupt my lunch."

"Sorry, Matt." The mechanical voice coming from the speaker didn't sound sorry. The inference was that a man in my condition could afford to have his lunch interrupted now and then. "Seth Borden is here to see you. I thought you might be interested."

I sat back for a moment, frowning. A trip to Las Vegas for Dickens' venerable Miss Havisham was easier to envision than a visit from Seth Borden. He was the last person in Roseacre I would have expected to need an attorney.

"Herd him in." I rewrapped the uneaten portion of my sandwich and put it away in the file drawer, sweeping crumbs in after it off the desk top. By that time my visitor was standing awkwardly just inside the door.

Seth was older than the woodwork in the office and looked it. Little and wizened—"elfin," the Sunday supplement writers would call him—he wore gold-rimmed spectacles on a bent nose, a white shirt, and fuzzy gray pin-striped trousers under a leather apron streaked liberally with grease. His face and his white tousled hair and his hands were no cleaner, the latter calloused and stained a permanent brown from the many compounds and acids with which he worked. He looked out of place, as he would have anywhere but amid the general disarray of his little workshop on Main Street.

I winched myself out of my chair and took his hand. It was warm and a little sticky. "Hello, Seth. Have a seat." I indicated the client's chair on his side of the desk.

He shook his head. "Can't stay. Got me some glue drying on two sticks of wood and can't let it set no longer'n ten minutes. I come to hire you, if you're in the mood for it." He fished a scrap of paper out of an apron pocket and handed it to me.

It was a subpoena ordering him to appear in court in two weeks to answer charges of diminished capacity filed by his daughter. Her name was typed at the bottom of the sheet: Mrs. C. Burton Scott. I gave it back. "What brought this on?"

"It's her husband put her up to it," he said. "When I refused to sell my shop to that developing firm of his, he got himself a lawyer and between them they cooked up this thing that says I'm crazy and should be committed. June always did do what Burton told her, so he got her to sign this here complaint. Once I'm out of the way, the shop's hers, and they can do what they want with it."

He seemed more sad than angry, which was like him. People like Seth Borden live their lives never believing they'll get hurt. They get hurt a lot. The scenario estmade sense. No one who lived in Roseacre could recall a time when Seth's shop wasn't there. Dwarfed though it was by skyscrapers the little brick structure occupied a substantial part of the business district and was worth hundreds of thousands to the developer fortunate enough to acquire it. Knowing what I did about C. Burton Scott, I wondered why I hadn't seen this coming.

Not that no one had tried before. Twenty years earlier, Bedelia Borden, Seth's sister and partner by grace of their father's will, had tried to bully Seth into selling her his half so that she could make a bundle from a man who wanted to buy up the block and build a department store. Her constant browbeating made her brother miserable and may have led to his wife Ruth's fatal heart attack at age forty-two. Bedelia might have won, having thus broken her brother's spirit, had not a severe recurrence of her childhood asthma forced her to abandon her interest and move to a dryer climate. No one had heard from her since and it was believed that she had died out west. Now the property was worth ten times what had been offered then.

The worst part was that in our state, the mere question of a person's sanity raised by his heirs was sufficient to go to court. Then it was a matter of which psychiatrist was more eloquent in expressing his opinions. Neither medicine nor the law is an exact science.

"Any reason to doubt your sanity, Seth?" I asked.

He shrugged, a gesture not calculated to win a lawyer's confidence. "I forget things. Who don't? But I pay my bills and I run my business and I don't keep my socks in the icebox like my uncle started doing just before he died. You think I'm crazy?" His eyes were sharp behind the spectacles.

"I'm not a psychiatrist. But I think I can help you. First I think we should discuss my fee."

Before I could continue, the old man reached into another pocket and came up with a fat handful of greasy, dog-eared bills, which he deposited atop my desk. I counted them. They came to twenty-three hundred dollars in twenties and fifties.

"I was saving for a new delivery van," he explained. "I'll be in the shop when you want me." He left, presumably to see to his two sticks of wood.

Mr. and Mrs. C. Burton Scott lived north of the city along Route 22, in one of a string of neat little homes with neat little lawns and big car in every driveway. I swung my Japanese puddle-jumper in behind a blue Seville and climbed out, sweating as soon as I left the air-conditioned interior. It was late August and fat men were out of season.

June Borden Scott answered the door on my second knock. She was a small woman of thirty, attractive enough, but there was too much of her Aunt Bedelia in her face to suit me. As a boy I had seen the old harridan once or twice and gone home feeling chilled. "Yes?" her voice was thin, almost non-existent.

I said, "I'm looking for Mr. Scott. Someone at his office said he was having lunch at home. I tried to call, but your number's unlisted. Matt Lysander. I think your husband remembers me."

He remembered me. Three seconds after June withdrew, he came storming up with fists clenched and stuck his big chin in my face. The rest of him was big, too, but I had eighty pounds on him, not that I cared to use them; he was all muscle. The shiny blue suits he always wore gave him an armored look. I'd noticed that in court, the day I persuaded a judge to fine Scott Developments fifty thousand dollars for using substandard materials in its construction. His appeal was still pending.

"What the hell do you want?" he demanded.

"Relax; this visit won't cost you a cent." Twisting the knife is one of my specialties. "I'm representing Seth Borden. Let's talk."

His expression changed from belligerent to uncertain. At length he stepped aside to admit me.

The living room was sunken, professionally decorated, and, I suspected, soundproof. I sat down in a brown crushed-leather chair without waiting for an invitation and stood my briefcase—an expensive prop on the floor next to it. Scott took a seat beside his wife on the sofa opposite, but he didn't relax. He sat on the edge as if crouched to spring. Mrs. Scott looked like a frightened hamster in his presence. She'd inherited nothing of her aunt's overbearing manner.

I began without preamble. "Mrs. Scott, what makes you think your father is senile?"

Her husband started to answer for her. I held up a hand and he closed his mouth.

"He's—well, he has lapses," she began haltingly. "I invite him to dinner and he doesn't show up. When I call him to find out why, he says he never received an invitation."

"How many times has this happened?"

"I don't know. Three times, I guess. Perhaps four. All in the past couple of months."

"That hardly indicates failing faculties," I commented.

"I've forgotten my share of invitations, mainly because I was too polite to say I didn't feel like going."

"Oh, but that's not all! Just last week when I was shopping, Father walked right past me on the street without stopping to say hello. I had to call him twice before he turned around and recognized me. His own daughter!"

"Perhaps he was preoccupied."

"What's he got to be preoccupied about in his world?" said Scott, sneering.

I ignored him. "Let me ask you this, Mrs. Scott. Were you concerned about your father's mental condition before you related these incidents to your husband?"

"Don't answer that!" Scott stood. His beefy face was red. "You can leave here on your feet or head first, Lysander. Your choice. I don't have to listen to this sort of thing in my own house."

"You will in court." I rose, facing him. "Let's be honest. All you've got is a couple of incidents of absentmindedness a first-year law student could tear apart, and even then it's just your word against Borden's. My psychiatrist will examine him, the state's psychiatrist will examine him, they'll both find exactly what they want to find, and they'll cancel each other out in court. In the end all you'll gain is a bill from your lawyer. Still want to go through with it?"

The obstinate expression remained on Scott's face, but his shoulders sank ever so slightly. "None of this would be necessary if the old fool would just sell." He was still angry, but not at me. "Did he tell you what I offered him for that pile of bricks?"

I said he hadn't. Scott quoted an amount. My surprise must have showed, because he inflated before my eyes.

"You see?" he roared. "Would you turn down a chance to retire and never have to worry about money for the rest of your life? Borden did, and without blinking. If that isn't evidence of diminished capacity, you tell me what is!"

I picked up my briefcase, composing myself. A lawyer's first duty is to do what he can to keep his client out of court, and I'd given it my best shot. "Don't say I didn't warn you when the judge speaks his piece."

Mrs. Scott accompanied me to the door. Her face showed strain.

"It's true what Burton said," she whispered. "He wouldn't have made an offer like that if it weren't my father. I know what you think of me. I'm sure it's what the whole town will be thinking when this gets out, but it isn't true. I just want to do what's best for Father, put him someplace where he won't harm himself. He won't move in here. I worry about him, all alone among those tools and things. You can see that, can't you?"

I went out without committing myself.

Back at my office, I asked Sharon to get Fred Petrillo on the line. Fred was an assistant to an assistant at the State Bureau of Records and he owed me a favor.

"Petrillo." His businesslike tone was romanticized by a strong Puerto Rican accent.

"Fred, this is Matt Lysander. Can you find out for me who C. Burton Scott's partners are over at Scott Developments?"

"I wasn't aware he had partners."

"Nor was I until about half an hour ago. A man who balks at a fifty thousand dollar fine doesn't make the kind of money offer that he just told me about without wincing. Someone's backing his play."

"I'll get right on it. Hour soon enough?"

"Dandy." I hung up and beat it down to Seth Borden's shop.

The proprietor was in back, refinishing an old desk that hardly seemed worth the bother. The floor around him was a litter of discarded tools under a mulch of wood shavings. A bare bulb swung from a cord above his head, slinging shadows over the cold walls. They weren't as ancient as they appeared. A couple of decades earlier, Seth had turned bricklayer and had redone the whole shop from top to bottom. But like everything else about him, his remodeling carried a built-in patina of age that a forger of art masterpieces would have given his artistic eye to duplicate.

After we had exchanged greetings, I asked Seth about his recent lapses. He scowled, sighting along the edge of a drawer he was sanding.

"I said before I forget things. And I didn't see June when I passed her. These here glasses are for close work. Sometimes

I don't get around to taking them off. I bet even the President does that now and then."

"One diminished capacity case at a time, please," I said. "Why'd you turn down Scott's offer?"

"Didn't want to sell. I said that." He resumed sanding.

"It's a lot of money. You could use it to buy a chain of shops and still take a trip around the world."

"I like it here."

"That's not good enough. This is a money-oriented society. It's going to look bad at the hearing when they ask you why you said no and that's the only answer you have."

He slid the drawer into place and straightened. "My father built this shop. I been working in it sixty years. There's still some things you can't buy."

"That's it?"

"That's the truth."

I let it go for the time being. Everybody lies to his lawyer. "Will you submit to a psychiatric examination?"

I asked. "The judge will insist on it. I've a friend, Dr. Casper Fyfe, with whom I've worked before. He's good."

"Do what feels right." He traded his spectacles for a pair of goggles and plugged in an electric sander. The noise drove me out of there.

"Brace yourself." Fred Petrillo sounded smug over the telephone. "Two years ago, controlling interest in Scott Developments was snapped up by Global Enterprises."

I replaced the receiver. I don't remember if I thanked him; I was in shock. Global Enterprises was a semi-legal subsidiary of that organization with a five-letter name beginning with M that we're not supposed to talk about anymore. It represented the organization's push to crack legitimate business, but from the number of vice-presidents who had shown up in automobile trunks at airports recently, it was clear that tactics hadn't changed since Prohibition. I filed the knowledge away for possible use later. At the time I had no reason to believe I'd need it soon.

Sharon showed Casper Fyfe in two days later. Grinning at her over the remains of my family-size pizza, I folded the cardboard, chucked it into the wastebasket, and grasped Casper's hand. She glared back and closed the door harder than necessary on the way out. Sharon was a fitness freak.

"You aren't losing any weight." Casper sat down.

I said, "I grow fat in the saddle, like Napoleon. What you got?"

"You won't like it." Lanky and balding, the psychiatrist wore the obligatory horn-rims and had a square jaw that must have offered a tempting target during his college boxing days. "In this doctor's opinion, Seth Borden is something less than stable."

"We should both be so crazy."

"I'm serious, Matt. You know I don't joke about my work."

My heart dropped a notch. "Give me the details."

"It isn't senility. He suffered a trauma somewhere in his past that drove him permanently off center. If I had a couple of years I could probably find it, but that won't help you."

"Just how screwy is he?"

"Psychiatrists don't recognize that term," he chided. "There's enough abnormality to provide Scott's attorney with plenty of ammunition. His heart's not too good either, judging by his color, but that's beside the point. Any testimony I gave would do your case more harm than good."

I sat back, deflated. "Well, that leaves only one way to go." I told him what I'd learned about Scott Developments.

"You think it will affect the judge's decision?"

"I don't know. It's an informal hearing, and Morton's presiding. He's emotional. Maybe a plot by the mob to gain a foot-hold in Roseacre will sway him our way. It's worth a shot."

"Good luck." Casper recommended a psychiatrist to refute the generalities advanced by the state shrink, after which we parted company. When he was gone I dialed Fred Petrillo at the capital for documentation to back up my forthcoming disclo-sure. The newspapers were going to fall in love with me.

The hearing went as I'd expected. Scott's lawyer scored points with the psychiatric testimony based on three visits with Seth Borden, a few of which I was able to knock down despite the handicap of my own expert's never having met the subject. I introduced Seth's ledger and balance sheets by way of showing that he was capable of operating his business. Judge Morton seemed unimpressed. At that point I'd hoped to present char-acter witnesses who could swear to the old man's stability, but it turned out he had no close friends. Scott's man rested his case. Then I brought out the big guns.

News that organized crime had its eye on Roseacre played hell with decorum. Spectators babbled excitedly. Scott leaped to his feet, cursing me. A photographer burst a flashbulb in my face. Morton's gavel handle cracked while he was pounding. I rested my case. The hearing was recessed until the afternoon.

When it convened again, Seth was absent. Scrubbed and wearing an old suit frayed at the cuffs, he had left after the morning session muttering something about work to do. I sent Johnny, one of my favorite gofers, to the old man's shop to see what was keeping him. After twenty minutes the boy returned, alone and white-faced. He whispered in my ear.

I rose. Morton's ice-blue eyes impaled me. "Your honor, I've just learned that my client, Seth Borden, is dead."

June Scott gasped. Then the tears came.

Her husband put an arm around her awkwardly. The gallery buzzed.

"He was found collapsed on the floor of his shop moments ago," I continued. "A doctor is there now. It looks as if Mr. Borden suffered a heart attack—brought on, perhaps, by the strain of this morning's proceedings."

Judge Morton adjourned the court.

Public outcry was fierce when June Scott acquired the building from probate, but since an autopsy definitely established natural causes in the old man's death and no criminal acts could be traced directly to Global Enterprises, the law withdrew. June lost no time in deeding the property over to Global Developments.

The day the shop was set to come down, Sharon put through a call from C. Burton Scott. He sounded upset.

"Meet me there, shyster." The receiver clicked in my ear.

The site was right around the corner from my office. I found Scott in hardhat and shiny blue suit standing outside a fence erected to keep out gawkers. His face was taut and pale. He seized my arm and steered me through the gate into the gutted shell of Seth's shop.

The wrecking crew had carted away everything worth salvaging, then gone to work with sledgehammers and crow-bars. I was dragged stumbling over bricks and broken mortar, past hardhatted workers standing around idle, to a gaping hole in the south wall. Scott let go of me to snatch a flashlight out of an employee's hand, switched it on. The hard white beam lanced the darkness inside the cavity.

I can't say I was surprised. The trauma in Seth's past, the extensive remodeling, his unwillingness to sell when he knew it would mean the shop's destruction, formed a pattern I worked with often. I hadn't said anything because there was nothing to be gained by doing so. That cost me trouble with the police later.

Dental records confirmed it after two days, but from the start there was no doubt that the broken skeleton lying crumpled in one corner of the ruined wall belonged to Bedelia Borden, Seth's money-mad sister, dead these twenty years.

CABANA

Hale thanked me for the glass of water and used it to chase down a yellow pill the size of a cuff link.

"I'm on medication," he told me helpfully. "I will be for the rest of my life, I guess. That's a tough admission to make at my age."

I figured that to be around twenty-five. He was a small, slender specimen with fragile wrists and features, and thick black hair cut short up front and long in the back, the way they're wearing it now. He looked healthy enough. He had the sinews of a runner under his tennis shirt and shorts.

"What've you got?" I refilled my glass from the pitcher of martinis on the wicker table, no pill.

"It has a Latin name I can't pronounce. As I understand it, it's a benign growth on my brain, hanging down like a stalagmite at the base of the occipital lobe. Without the medication, any exertion or great shock can cause it to move and touch my spinal column. I black out. Afterward I can't remember anything from a few minutes before the blackout. I'm told I become abusive, even violent."

"And with the medication?"

"I'm a little better. Do you know where Sharon is, Mr. Gardener?"

I looked past him at the ocean. Nothing new there.

At that hour of the afternoon it was teal-blue, the long swells coming in like wind blowing across satin and creaming on the beach. I'd been living in the little cabana behind me for two years and nothing ever changed, not the ocean or the throbbing blue sky or the growling and honking of Rio beyond the palms on the hill.

"I found her," I said, "I think. I've sent someone to confirm the address. Come back tomorrow morning and I'll have it for you."

He gulped down the rest of his water. "I was told you work alone."

"I farm out some of the grunt work. Don't worry, he doesn't know about Detroit."

"I shouldn't have told you. I still don't know how you got it out of me."

"Relax. There's no extradition between the United States and Brazil. At least half the people I work for are thieves. Most of them are like you, amateurs who embezzled a bundle in one shot and took off with the briefcase for romantic Rio. Amateur thieves fall into patterns. I needed to know she was one before I started looking."

"Sharon isn't a thief," he said. "Not really. I took that money. She didn't even know about it until we were in the air, on our way to a two-week vacation in South America, or so she thought."

"Plenty of women here. Why bring her at all?"

"We were going to be married. We still are, if I can find her and apologize. I—had an episode. In the Rio de Janeiro airport. I woke up in jail. The officers told me I tried to tear the place apart. Sharon was gone. So was the suitcase and six hundred thousand dollars."

"And you want to apologize to her?"

"I must have frightened her. She never saw one of my spells before. I was nervous, forgot to take my medication. That was two weeks ago. She must be terrified, with all that money in a strange country and no way to get back home. She'd be afraid to buy a ticket with stolen bills."

My glass was empty again; evaporation's a problem in Brazil. I filled it again and drank. I felt the familiar gnawing at my ulcer. "Is it her you want, or the money?"

"Both. I love Sharon, but I threw away my career for the money. What good's a career if this tumor turns malignant? If I'm going to die young, I want it to be in a villa overlooking the ocean with the woman I love at my side."

"Romantic. Come back tomorrow morning."

The sun was barely over the sill when someone banged on the cabana door. I stumbled to the window in my shorts and looked out at Hale standing on the little flagged patio where we'd sat the previous afternoon. The pitcher with its puddle of melted ice looked sad.

"Have you got it?" he demanded when I opened the door. Today he had on a Sea Island shirt over white flannels.

I gave him the address. "It belongs to a cabana like this one. It's a twenty-minute drive down the coast. Want me to go with you?"

"No, thanks." He handed me an envelope full of cash. He watched me count it. "Are you all right, Gardener? You look like hell."

"Damn ulcers kept me up all night."

"You ought to give up drinking."

"What else is there to do down here?"

He thanked me for my good work and left. The wheels of his rented Jeep spun and spat sand.

I gave him five minutes, then dressed and went after him in my Mexican Oldsmobile.

The cabana was about the same size as mine, but nicer, with a red Spanish tile roof and recent white paint on the stucco. There was a little flower garden in front, professionally tended. Nice view of the ocean out back. Apparently Sharon didn't mind spending stolen money on overhead as much as she did using it to buy a ticket home; but that had been Hale's assessment, and he was no judge of character. His Jeep was parked in front.

The front door stood wide open. Inside, the place looked like hurricane footage: furniture dumped over, cushions slashed and bleeding white cotton batting, holes kicked in the plaster. Hale was sitting on the floor in the middle of it all, next to the woman's body. She had on a halter top, shorts, and sandals. She had been a pretty blonde before someone had caved in her face with something hard and heavy.

He looked up at me. I could see his skull through his pale skin. "Did I—? Did I—?"

"Black out? I guess so." I leaned down, felt the woman's throat, and wiped my hand on my pants. "She's dead, okay. You want to tell me anything?"

"I don't remember. I don't—I wouldn't hurt Sharon."

I said nothing. He saw where I was looking and glanced down at the object in his hand. It was a stone carving of one of the Inca gods like you find in the better Souvenir shops, plastered with blood. He dropped it as if it had suddenly sprung to life.

"That'd do it," I said, nodding. "You'd better get up. We'll figure out something to tell the cops. They're down on *norté-americanos* here, importing their troubles to peaceful Brazil." I held out my hand.

He stared at it for a moment, as a dog will. Then he grasped it.

He was almost upright when I stuck the little Czech automatic into his belly and pulled the trigger three times.

The cabana had no telephone, so I walked down the beach and gave a dollar to one of the boys who sell maps to Pizarro's sunken gold to fetch an officer. Then I went back inside to wait.

I hadn't counted on the shock of his finding Sharon's battered body triggering one of Hale's blackouts, but it didn't matter. Even if he never remembered being innocent of her murder, he wouldn't forget the money. I'd spent most of the night looking for it after I'd killed her, and had only just gotten back to my cabana with it and undressed for bed when he banged on the door. It was a good set-up, considering how little time I'd had to rig it after I found out about Hale's condition. The medical examiners in Rio de Janeiro are among the best in the world; once a thorough autopsy brought his tumor to light, I'd have no trouble convincing the authorities I'd shot him in self-defense when he attacked me after bludgeoning the girl to death in one of his blind rages.

By the time they found out about the six hundred thousand, I'd be out of this country, with its unchanging sky and monotonous surf and too many thieves.

ABOUT THE AUTHOR

Loren D. Estleman is a critically acclaimed author of historical crime and Western fiction with over eighty published books. He graduated from Eastern Michigan University in 1974 with a Bachelor of Arts degree in English literature and journalism. His first novel, *The Oklahoma Punk*, was published in 1976. In 1980, he published the first novel of the Amos Walker series, which he is most known for, *Motor City Blue*. He has received twenty-two national writing awards, including an Owen Wister Award for lifetime achievement and two American Mystery Awards, and has been nominated for the National Book Award and the Edgar Award.

He currently lives in Michigan with his wife, Deborah Morgan.

LOREN D. ESTLEMAN

FROM OPEN ROAD MEDIA

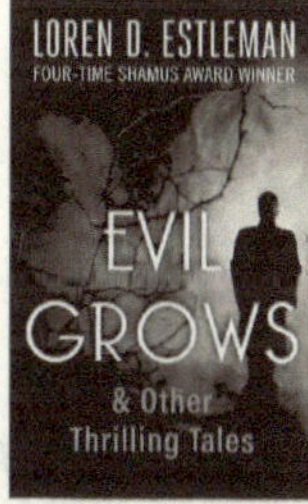

Find a full list of our authors and
titles at www.openroadmedia.com

FOLLOW US
@OpenRoadMedia

www.ingramcontent.com/pod-product-compliance
Lightning Source LLC
Chambersburg PA
CBHW020807310726
48969CB00002B/745